# "Picard to Commander Riker."

The only answer was static. *"Enterprise* to away team—respond!"

At that moment the lights on the bridge began to flicker, and consoles started going dark one after another.

"Sir!" shouted Hawk, the lieutenant at conn, "command control is being rerouted to Main Engineering! Weapons, shields—"

"Data," ordered Picard, "quickly—lock out the main computer!"

The android rushed to a console, and his fingers were a blur as they worked the controls. Within seconds, he was finished.

"I have isolated the main computer with an encryption code," explained Data. "It is highly unlikely the Borg will be able to break it."

More lights went out. "The Borg have cut power to all decks," reported Worf, "except Sixteen."

"But without the computer," said Hawk, "they won't be able to control the ship."

"The Borg won't stay on Deck Sixteen," said Picard with certainty.

**Star Trek: The Next Generation**
**STARFLEET ACADEMY**

#1 Worf's First Adventure
#2 Line of Fire
#3 Survival
#4 Capture the Flag
#5 Atlantis Station
#6 Mystery of the Missing Crew
#7 Secret of the Lizard People
#8 Starfall
#9 Nova Command
#10 Loyalties
#11 Crossfire

**Star Trek:**
**STARFLEET ACADEMY**

#1 Crisis on Vulcan
#2 Aftershock
#3 Cadet Kirk

**Star Trek: Deep Space Nine**

#1 The Star Ghost
#2 Stowaways
#3 Prisoners of Peace
#4 The Pet
#5 Arcade
#6 Field Trip
#7 Gypsy World
#8 Highest Score

**Star Trek movie tie-ins**

Star Trek Generations
Star Trek First Contact

Available from MINSTREL Books

# STAR TREK®
# FIRST CONTACT™

**A Special Young Adult Novelization by
John Vornholt**
based on the film STAR TREK: FIRST CONTACT
Story by Rick Berman & Brannon Braga & Ronald D. Moore
Screenplay by Brannon Braga & Ronald D. Moore

A
MINSTREL®
BOOK

Published by POCKET BOOKS
New York   London   Toronto   Sydney   Tokyo   Singapore

A MINSTREL PAPERBACK *Original*

A Minstrel Book published by
POCKET BOOKS, a division of Simon & Schuster Inc.
1230 Avenue of the Americas, New York, NY 10020

STAR TREK is a Registered Trademark of Paramount Pictures.

A VIACOM COMPANY

This book is published by Pocket Books, a division of Simon & Schuster Inc., under exclusive license from Paramount Pictures.

ISBN: 0-671-00128-0

First Minstrel Books printing December 1996

10 9 8 7 6 5 4 3 2 1

A MINSTREL BOOK and colophon are registered trademarks of Simon & Schuster Inc.

Printed in the U.S.A.

*For Cassie, Tom, and Brenna*

# STARFLEET TIMELINE

## 2264

The launch of Captain James T. Kirk's five-year mission, _U.S.S. Enterprise,_ NCC-1701.

## 2292

Alliance between the Klingon Empire and the Romulan Star Empire collapses.

## 2293

Colonel Worf, grandfather of Worf Rozhenko, defends Captain Kirk and Doctor McCoy at their trial for the murder of Klingon chancellor Gorkon.

Khitomer Peace Conference, Klingon Empire/Federation (_Star Trek VI_).

## 2323

Jean-Luc Picard enters Starfleet Academy's standard four-year program.

## 2328

The Cardassian Empire annexes the Bajoran homeworld.

## 2346

Romulan massacre of Klingon outpost on Khitomer.

## 2351

In orbit around Bajor, the Cardassians construct a space station that they will later abandon.

## 2363

Captain Jean-Luc Picard assumes command of _U.S.S. Enterprise,_ NCC-1701-D.

## 2367

Wesley Crusher enters Starfleet Academy.

An uneasy truce is signed between the Cardassians and the Federation.

Borg attack at Wolf 359; First Officer Lieutenant Commander Benjamin Sisko and his son, Jake, are among the survivors.

U.S.S. Enterprise-D defeats the Borg vessel in orbit around Earth.

## 2369

Commander Benjamin Sisko assumes command of Deep Space Nine in orbit over Bajor.

## 2371

U.S.S. Enterprise, NCC-1701-D, destroyed on Veridian III.

Former Enterprise captain James T. Kirk emerges from a temporal nexus, but dies helping Picard save the Veridian system.

U.S.S. Voyager, under the command of Captain Kathryn Janeway, is accidentally transported to the Delta Quadrant. The crew begins a 70-year journey back to Federation space.

## 2372

The Klingon Empire's attempted invasion of Cardassia Prime results in the dissolution of the Khitomer peace treaty between the Federation and the Klingon Empire.

Source: Star Trek® Chronology / Michael Okuda and Denise Okuda

# STAR TREK®
## FIRST CONTACT™

# CHAPTER 1

The dark shadowy chamber was huge, and it was filled with coffin-sized boxes, rows upon rows of them. They covered the walls, the floor, and even the ceiling. Inside each box was a cyborg with black machinery attached to his face and body. There must have been thousands of them!

Captain Jean-Luc Picard stared at the creatures. Even standing perfectly still, they were frightening. He smelled something dank and moist, and he heard mechanical clicks and dripping noises. And voices— a million voices filled his head, all babbling at once.

Picard knew that he was inside the Borg Collective, and the memory chilled his spine. In all this black- ness, there was only one bit of color—a red Starfleet uniform hanging in the corner.

Suddenly he was hurtling along a corridor, past more and more silent Borg. They lined the walls, looking like vampires in their coffins. Picard was slammed on top of an operating table. He struggled to escape, but the Borg put straps on his arms and legs. Roughly they grabbed his head and held it down.

A needle-sharp probe began to move toward his face, and he could see it coming closer and closer. He struggled and struggled, but there was no escape. Just when he thought the needle would pierce his eye, a woman's face hovered over him.

Her skin was ghostly pale, and her lips looked drained of life. In a low raspy voice, she said, "Locutus."

Then Picard saw his own face—it was gray, lifeless, and half-covered with Borg machinery. "I am Locutus of Borg," he answered. "Resistance is futile."

"No!" Picard screamed as he woke up, sweating and panting. With relief, he realized that he was seated at his desk in his ready room, aboard the *Enterprise-E*. It was all just a nightmare! Picard didn't know what had come over him. He figured that he had better splash some water on his face and wake up.

The captain rose from his desk, straightened his uniform, and walked to the bathroom. That had been a terrifying nightmare, and he tried not to think about it. He hadn't dreamed about the Borg—and his experience with them—for a long time. Why now?

He stopped in front of the sink and stuck his hands under the faucet, which turned on the water. Picard splashed the soothing liquid on his face and gazed absently at his reflection in the mirror. He began to relax, glad to be awake and thinking clearly again.

As he looked at his face, a muscle in his cheek twitched slightly, and he heard a strange chirping sound.

Desperately, Picard rubbed his cheek to try to make the muscle stop twitching, but it wouldn't stop! Suddenly a Borg servo punched through his cheek and whirred at him. Picard gasped and bolted upright.

This time the captain found himself seated on his couch in his quarters aboard the *Enterprise-E*. He wanted to believe that he was truly awake, but that maddening chirp kept ringing in his ear. Picard whirled toward his desk and saw that a message was coming in over his computer terminal.

He let out a sharp breath and decided that he had better get control of himself. With determination, Picard walked to the terminal and studied the readout:

"Incoming transmission. Starfleet Command to Captain J. L. Picard, *U.S.S. Enterprise NCC-1701-E*. Command authorization required."

The captain collected himself and tapped the panel. "Authorization: Picard," he said, "four-seven-alpha-tango."

The screen shifted to the familiar Starfleet insignia on its peaceful blue background, and the captain tensed once more. If a Borg suddenly came on the screen, he was going to stop sleeping altogether.

But it was Admiral Hayes, who looked as serious as a Borg.

"Admiral," said Picard, trying to sound calm.

"Catch you at a bad time, Jean-Luc?" asked Hayes.

"No, of course not," lied Picard.

"I just received a disturbing report from Deep Space Twelve," began the admiral. "Long-range sensors have picked up—"

Picard's jaw tightened. He knew exactly what the admiral was going to say next. *They* had already told him in his dream.

"I know," said the captain gravely. "The Borg."

A few minutes later Captain Picard stood in the spacious observation lounge of the new *Enterprise,* gazing at the vast starscape beyond the windows. Picard usually took comfort from the great distances of space, but not today. No matter how vast it was, space couldn't protect them from a terrifying enemy.

He glanced at the walls, which were decorated with previous *Enterprise* models. The *Enterprise-E* was part of a long proud line that stretched back to primitive shuttles and sailing vessels. He liked this room because it conveyed that sense of history and tradition.

The door whooshed open, and in walked his trusted staff of officers. Commander Will Riker was in the lead, a pleasant smile on his bearded face. Then came Data, the one-of-a-kind android, followed by the ship's counselor, Deanna Troi. Arriving a few steps after them came his old friend, Dr. Beverly Crusher, and the chief engineer, Geordi La Forge.

Geordi no longer wore his familiar VISOR over his sightless eyes. He now had electronic ocular implants that worked as well as the bulky VISOR had. Geordi had patiently waited for just the right upgrade before giving up his VISOR, and Picard was happy that his choice had worked out so well.

The captain paused a moment, expecting to see Lieutenant Commander Worf come striding in. Then he remembered—Worf had transferred to Deep Space Nine to advise Captain Sisko about the hostilities between the Klingons and the Cardassians. Well, they certainly didn't need the big Klingon for their present assignment.

After his officers had gathered around the large conference table, Picard told them what Admiral Hayes had told him. He waited for their response.

"How many Borg ships?" asked Geordi.

"One," answered Picard. "And it's on a direct course for Earth. It will cross the Federation border in less than an hour."

Riker shifted uneasily in his chair, anxious to be doing something about this threat. Picard didn't blame him, but he wanted to assure his officers that something *was* being done.

"Admiral Hayes has begun mobilizing a fleet in the Typhon Sector," explained Picard. "He hopes to stop the Borg before they reach Earth."

Data cocked his head. "At maximum warp, it will take us three hours, twenty-five minutes to reach—"

"We're not going," Picard interrupted.

Everyone gaped at him. If possible, they were more stunned by this news than the report that the Borg were threatening Earth.

"What do you mean, we're not going?" asked Deanna Troi.

Picard's lips thinned. "Our orders are to patrol the Neutral Zone, in case the Romulans try to take advantage of the situation."

"The *Romulans?*" asked Troi, puzzled.

"Captain," said Data, "there has been no unusual activity along the Romulan border for the past nine months. It seems highly unlikely that they would choose this moment to start a conflict."

Beverly glanced at the captain and said, "Maybe Starfleet feels we haven't had enough shakedown time."

*Nice try, Beverly,* thought Picard. *We both know that's not the real reason.*

Geordi shook his head in amazement. "We've been in space for nearly a year. We're ready. The *Enterprise-E* is the most advanced starship in the fleet. We should be in the front lines!"

"I've voiced all of these concerns to Starfleet Command," said the captain. "Their orders stand."

A profound silence gripped the room. Even in the blackness of space, it couldn't have been more silent.

"Number One, set course for the Neutral Zone." With that order, Captain Picard left the room. He couldn't stand looking at their shocked faces any longer.

\*   \*   \*

Several hours later Captain Picard stood in his ready room, staring out his window at a different sprinkling of stars upon a different stretch of emptiness. This was the Romulan Neutral Zone, which was normally a trouble spot. With the battle elsewhere, being here today felt like a walk in the park. Or a retreat.

Picard sipped a cup of Earl Grey tea as a Berlioz opera blasted at full volume behind him. Neither one was calming him. In a reflection off the window, he saw Commander Riker stride through the door. The captain turned around to see his first officer frowning at the loud music.

"Wagner?" asked Riker uncertainly.

"Berlioz," said the captain curtly. "What do you have?"

Riker handed him a computer padd. "We finished our first sensor sweep of the Neutral Zone."

Picard took the handheld device and studied the readouts for a moment. He muttered, "Fascinating. Twenty particles of space dust per cubic meter, fifty-two ultraviolet radiation spikes, and a class-two comet. This is certainly worthy of our time."

With disgust, the captain tossed the padd onto a side table.

"Captain, why are we out here chasing comets?" demanded Riker.

Picard narrowed his eyes. "Let's just say that Starfleet has every confidence in the *Enterprise* and her crew. But they're not so sure about her captain."

He shook his fist and paced the length of the room.

7

"They believe that a man who was once captured by the Borg, and assimilated, should not be put in a situation where he would face them again. To do so would be to introduce an 'unstable element into a critical situation.'"

Riker stared at him with a mixture of shock and anger. "That's crazy. Your experience with the Borg makes you the perfect man to lead this fight."

"Admiral Hayes disagrees," said Picard.

Before either man could say another word, Troi's voice broke in over the captain's comm badge. "Bridge to Captain Picard."

"Go ahead," he answered.

"We've just received word from Starfleet Command. They've engaged the Borg."

Riker glanced worriedly at him, and the captain led the way onto the bridge.

He nodded to Troi and noted with satisfaction that he had his best crew on duty, with Data at the Ops console and Lieutenant Hawk on Conn. On the *Enterprise-E,* a single command chair dominated the room, and Picard liked how the surrounding stations faced inward instead of out. That gave him face-to-face access to his officers.

As he crossed to his chair, he ordered, "Mr. Data, put Starfleet subspace frequency one-four-eight-six on audio."

"Aye, sir."

Picard sat in his command chair and watched Data work his console. They heard bits of static-filled communication from the distant battle, and there were grave expressions all around. The Borg were the most ruthless enemy the Federation had ever faced, and the bridge crew knew it.

Finally the voices on the audio link became clear enough to understand: "Flagship to *Endeavor,* stand by to engage at grid A-fifteen. *Defiant* and *Bozeman,* fall back to mobile position one."

"Acknowledged."

"We have it in visual range—a Borg cube! On course zero mark two-one-five; speed, warp nine-point-eight—"

An eerie Borg voice broke in. "We are the Borg. Lower your shields and surrender your ships." To Picard, the voice sounded like thousands of voices speaking as one.

The monotone voice continued, "We will add your biological and technological distinctiveness to our own. Your culture will adapt to service us. Resistance is futile. We are the Borg."

There was static, and a Starfleet voice cut in, "All units, open fire! Remodulate shield nutation."

Terrible sounds filled the air, and the officer's voice came back in a panic. "We're losing power . . . warp core breach . . . all hands abandon ship!"

A horrible explosion sounded over the audio link, which made everyone jump. The voices that cut in were more urgent now. "This is the flagship! They've broken through the defense perimeter—they're heading toward Earth! Pursuit course! Break off the attack and—"

Picard scowled. He had heard enough, and he

signaled to Data to end the transmission. Tense silence filled the bridge, and everyone was looking at him, wondering what he would do next.

He didn't leave them waiting long. "Lieutenant Hawk, set course for Earth. Maximum warp."

There were some surprised looks, but Riker gave him a nod of approval. Picard spoke to everyone on the bridge. "I am about to commit a direct violation of our orders. Any of you who wish to object, do so now, and I'll note it in my log."

The crew glanced at one another, but no one objected. Data, however, looked up at him. "I think I speak for everyone here, sir, when I say—forget our orders."

Picard smiled briefly at the rebellious android, then he was all business. "Red alert. All hands to battle stations."

A Klaxon sounded, and the bridge shifted to running lights, as people scrambled into action. Picard dropped into his chair and pointed at Lieutenant Hawk.

"Engage."

The sleek *Enterprise-E*—one of the fastest, most powerful starships ever built by Starfleet—zoomed into warp drive. The stars blurred as space stretched beyond the speed of light.

# CHAPTER 2

With its wispy clouds and blue seas, Earth looked as harmless as a beach ball floating in a dark pool. Streaking toward the peaceful planet came a giant cube, the size of a small moon. Strange machinery covered the Borg vessel, making it look like an alien puzzle box.

Suddenly the stern of the cube was raked by a barrage of torpedoes, and sparks rippled along its massive hull. A dozen Starfleet warships came into view, chasing the Borg ship and firing at will. But they were like gnats on a bull. The Borg cube never strayed from its course—straight toward Earth.

From an array of weapons spread across its hull, the cube fired back on its pursuers. Scores of pinpoint rays and torpedoes hammered the Starfleet vessels.

One big cruiser erupted in a fireball, sending wreckage spiraling in every direction. Another starship burst into sparks and went dark, coasting lifelessly in space.

Dodging among the crippled vessels was a compact prototype warship, the *Defiant.* It didn't escape damage, however, as a brace of Borg torpedoes slammed into it. Somehow the little ship righted itself and fired back with a burst of its own phasers.

On the bridge of the *Defiant,* conditions were desperate. Most of the consoles lay in ruin, and sparks and smoke spewed into the air. The deck was littered with debris and injured crew members, and people were coughing and groaning.

Lieutenant Commander Worf shook off the dizziness from a blow to his head. He touched his forehead, feeling blood. This was indeed a worthy battle and a worthy adversary. He reached up, grabbed a smoldering console, and hauled himself to his feet.

"Report!" barked the Klingon.

His Conn officer gasped for breath. "Main power's off-line. We've lost shields and our weapons are gone!"

Worf looked pleased for a moment. "Perhaps today is a good day—to die. Ramming speed!"

"Sir, there's another starship coming in!" The Conn officer blinked in amazement at his readouts. "It's the *Enterprise!*"

Worf frowned in surprise. "Perhaps the battle is not lost."

\* \* \*

Like David facing Goliath, the sleek *Enterprise* soared toward the massive cube, unleashing a storm of phaser fire. The Borg vessel shifted its fire from the crippled ships to the *Enterprise,* rocking the new vessel at point-blank range. Its shields absorbed most of the damage.

On the bridge of the *Enterprise,* Captain Picard clenched his fists and glanced at his trusted officers. They knew they were facing death, yet not one of them flinched from the duties at hand.

Riker said, "The *Defiant*'s losing life support!"

Picard tapped his comm panel. "Bridge to Transporter Room Three—beam the *Defiant* survivors aboard."

"Captain," said the first officer, "the flagship's been destroyed."

Picard nodded grimly. "What's the status on the Borg cube?"

"It has sustained heavy damage on its outer hull," answered Data. "I am reading fluctuations in their power grid."

"On screen," ordered the captain.

The incredible image of the Borg cube filled the holographic viewscreen, and Picard stood and walked toward it. Faintly he heard the agitated voices of the Borg inside his mind. Yes, they were in trouble. They could be finished with decisive action.

"Number One," he ordered, "open a channel to the other Starfleet vessels."

As Riker opened the channel, the captain moved to Data's console and checked the coordinates. He punched in commands to broadcast them to the surviving Federation ships.

"This is Captain Picard of the *Enterprise*," he said into the open channel. "I'm taking command of the fleet. Target every weapon you have on the following coordinates, and fire on my command."

Data frowned slightly. "Captain, the coordinates you have indicated do not appear to be a vital system."

"Trust me, Data."

"The fleet's ready," said Riker tensely.

"Fire," answered Picard.

Every Federation ship in the vicinity opened fire at once. A withering wave of phasers and torpedoes blasted a single spot on the Borg cube. The hull sizzled for a moment, then began to crack—even the massive Borg ship couldn't withstand such a concentrated attack.

The cube exploded in a titanic blast, sending flame, gas, and debris hurtling in every direction.

Picard watched this on his viewscreen, feeling a sense of triumph. But the joy was short-lived. Out of the cloud of gas and flame came a small gray sphere. It flashed past the viewscreen and kept going.

The captain whirled toward the Conn. "Pursuit course. Engage."

As Hawk worked his console to reverse their course, Captain Picard returned to his chair. His troubled expression brought Counselor Troi to his side.

"What?" she whispered.

He didn't answer, because he didn't want to give

voice to his worst fear—that he had done exactly what the Borg wanted him to do.

The turbolift doors opened, and Beverly Crusher entered, wearing a faint smile. "I have a patient here who insisted on coming to the bridge."

Before Picard could object, Worf entered. His uniform looked torn and singed, and there was a smear of dried blood on his forehead. Otherwise, he looked hale and hearty. The captain rushed to greet his old comrade.

"Welcome to the *Enterprise-E,* Mr. Worf."

"Thank you, sir," replied the Klingon. "The *Defiant*—?"

Picard glanced at a nearby console. "Adrift . . . but salvageable."

"Tough little ship," said Riker.

"Little?" Worf glared at his old friend, and they both broke into smiles.

"We could use some help at Tactical, Worf," said Picard.

"Of course." Worf moved to the tactical station, which was larger and more spread out than his old post on the *Enterprise-D.*

Riker sidled over and whispered, "You do remember how to fire phasers?"

Worf looked puzzled. "It's the green button, right?"

Riker smiled and moved away.

"I have the Borg sphere on visual," said Data.

"On screen," ordered Picard.

The viewscreen blinked on, and they could see the metallic sphere still hurtling toward the planet Earth.

"Sensors show chronometric particles emanating from the sphere," reported Data.

Picard stared at the screen. "They're creating a temporal vortex—"

"Time travel?" asked Riker.

The Borg sphere began to glow, turning bright red as it encountered friction in the Earth's atmosphere. Just ahead of it, a maelstrom of pulsing, swirling energy formed a hole in space. The sphere shot into the shifting vortex like a ball dropping into a magical lake, and a splash of energy radiated outward.

The *Enterprise* was rocked by the wave of energy. The viewscreen went dark, the lights flickered, and everybody staggered to stay on their feet.

"We're caught in some kind of temporal wake!" shouted Riker. A moment later the trembling subsided, and the viewscreen came back on.

Deanna Troi gasped. "Captain—the Earth!"

Everyone turned to look at the viewscreen. The energy wake was thinning to reveal Earth, but this wasn't the same Earth. The blue beach ball was now dark and turbulent, as if choked by a polluted atmosphere. The vortex remained opened, and in its spinning center, they could see the real Earth—blue and healthy.

Data reported, "The atmosphere contains high concentrations of methane, carbon monoxide, and fluorine."

"Lifesigns?" asked Picard.

"Population, approximately nine billion," answered Data. "All Borg."

Picard's shoulders slumped. In shock, Deanna turned to him. "But how?" she asked.

"They must've done it in the past," answered Picard as he stared at the gray lifeless planet. "They went back and assimilated Earth—changed history."

Beverly shook her head. "But if they changed history, why are *we* still here?"

"The temporal wake must have protected us from changes in the time line," surmised Data. With another glance at his console, he added, "The vortex is collapsing."

Everyone stared at Captain Picard. "Data, hold your course," he ordered, moving toward his chair. "We have to follow them back . . . repair whatever damage they've done."

Just as the swirling vortex began to close, cutting off the past from the future, the *Enterprise* soared into it. A moment later both were gone, leaving only the gray mechanized Borg planet, once known as Earth.

# CHAPTER

# 3

On a cold Montana night, people wandered into a bar called the Crash and Burn, drawn by the rock music blasting from its jukebox. The bar was the busiest place in the makeshift town, which was built on the remains of an old missile complex.

It was a ramshackle collection of prefab huts, tents, and radar dishes, decorated with homemade signs and banners. There wasn't much to do in the town, but the ex-soldiers and drifters came for the shelter, and a sense of community. The war had taken everything else.

Zefram Cochrane and Lily Sloane stepped out of the bar and walked slowly down the street. The lanky gray-haired man had his arm draped around Lily, and a stiff breeze also held him up. Cochrane was a little drunk.

He smiled at his companion, but she scowled at him. Cochrane liked Lily, because she was smart, pretty, and had a good sense of humor. *But watch out for her temper,* he told himself. He could put up with it, as long as she kept finding the parts he needed.

Lily liked him, too, or so he thought. Maybe it was just the promise of making a lot of money that kept her close. Well, thought Cochrane, by tomorrow they would be either rich, or dead. They would be worth millions, or they would be space junk. No wonder he wanted to get drunk.

"You're going to regret this," Lily warned him.

Cochrane looked indignantly at her. "If there's one thing you should've learned about me by now, young lady . . . it's that I have no regrets. Come on, Lily, one more round!"

He tried to reverse course to the bar, but Lily steered him back toward his tent. "You've had enough. I'm not riding in that thing tomorrow with a drunken pilot."

Cochrane grunted and wanted to tell her that he wasn't a very good pilot, even when he was sober. But Lily was staring into the starlit sky. "What is that?" she asked.

He looked up and tried to focus his eyes. "That, my dear, is the constellation Leo."

"No, that!"

She pointed him in the right direction, and he did

see something fairly strange. A bright light swept across the starlit sky, then it stopped and hovered above the missile complex. Two streaks of light erupted from the sphere and hit the town, resulting in huge explosions.

The ground shuddered from the force of the blasts, and Cochrane and Lily scurried for cover. The mysterious glowing ball kept firing, ripping up the town and sending people screaming into the night. As smoke and debris rained down upon them, Cochrane tried to find a place to hide.

"After all these years!" Cochrane gasped. He was suddenly sober.

"You think it's the ECON?" asked Lily.

"They couldn't have waited another day?"

Explosions rocked the ground all around them, and they huddled together fearfully.

"We've got to get to the *Phoenix!*" wailed Lily. She jumped to her feet and headed for the missile silo, but Cochrane was frozen with fear.

He watched her running across the compound, doing what he was supposed to be doing—but he couldn't brave the explosions! What he needed was a drink.

"Forget the *Phoenix!*" Cochrane grumbled to himself. He jumped to his feet and ran for the bar.

On the bridge of the *Enterprise,* Captain Picard gripped the arms of his chair until the shaking stopped. They were finally coming out of the temporal vortex.

"Report."

Riker answered, "Shields are down, long-range sensors are off-line, but main power's holding."

"According to our astrometric readings," said Data, "we are in the mid-twenty-first century. From the radioactive isotopes in the atmosphere, I would estimate we have arrived approximately ten years after the Third World War."

"That makes sense," said Riker. "Most of the major cities were destroyed . . . only a few governments left . . . six hundred million dead. No resistance."

"Captain!" shouted Worf. He pointed to the viewscreen.

Everyone followed the Klingon's gaze to see the Borg sphere pumping photon torpedoes at the surface of Earth.

"Quantum torpedoes!" ordered Picard. "Fire when ready!"

Worf swiftly entered the commands, and a brace of torpedoes were launched. Picard watched the screen as the torpedoes slammed into the sphere, and it exploded with a blast that lit up the night sky.

As the *Enterprise* was rocked by the shockwave, Picard turned to his first officer. "They were firing at the surface. Where?"

Riker queried the short-range scanners. "Western hemisphere," he answered. "North American continent. It looks like some sort of missile complex in central Montana."

"'Missile complex,'" repeated Picard. He wracked

his brain for any historical reference to Montana. Finally it came to him! "The date, Data? I need to know the exact date."

"The date is April fourth, 2063," answered the android.

Picard looked at Riker, and the first officer's eyes widened. "April fourth . . . that's one day before First Contact!"

"Precisely," answered Data.

"That's what they came here to do," said Picard grimly, "stop First Contact."

Beverly strode to his side. "If that's true, then the missile complex must be where *Zefram Cochrane* is building his warp ship!"

"How much damage did they do?" Picard asked quickly.

"Can't tell," answered Riker. "Long-range sensors are still off-line."

The captain did not hesitate as he made his decision. "We have to go down there and find out what happened."

He rushed toward the turbolift. "Data, Beverly, you're with me. Number One, have a security team meet us in Transporter Room Three. We need twenty-first-century civilian clothes. You have the bridge."

"Yes, sir," answered Riker.

Picard, Data, Beverly, and four security officers materialized near the perimeter of a large missile silo. They were wearing civilian clothes, with their comm badges well hidden inside their jackets. The security officers drew their phasers, and Data and Beverly opened their tricorders.

The captain led the way around a large smoking crater caused by the Borg fire. A moment later the away team reached thick concrete doors that protected the missile silo. Picard was about to order phaser fire on the doors when he spotted a stairway leading down.

"There," he said, taking the lead.

They found the door open, and they explored underground passageways until Picard found the control room. Unlike most of the silo, this room had working equipment, although much of it was damaged in the attack. Under the wreckage lay three bodies.

"They're all dead," reported Beverly, studying her medical tricorder.

Picard nodded grimly, fearing that they were too late. He glanced at the monitors, computers, and tracking equipment, thinking that Data's tricorder could probably replace all of it.

"See if Cochrane is one of these people," he told Beverly. "Data, let's check on the warp ship."

The captain and the android hurried out a different door and found themselves in a long narrow passageway. They walked down the corridor until they came to thick concrete doors. *Blast doors,* thought Picard. They shielded the people in the complex from the missile's booster rockets.

Picard nodded to Data, and they went inside. Now

they found themselves on a metal catwalk in a large circular room. Picard led the way to the center of the silo, and he gasped when he got his first look at it— Zefram Cochrane's warp ship!

It looked more like an advanced ICBM missile than a starship, with a cockpit instead of a warhead. There were other refinements, but it still looked like a crude rocket ship.

Written on the side of the famous vessel was the name *Phoenix*. Picard also saw scorch marks and dents on the fuselage, which worried him. There were catwalks on the lower levels, so that workers had access to all parts of the ship.

Data studied his tricorder. "There is significant damage to the fuselage and primary intercooler system."

Picard nodded. "We should have the original blueprints in the *Enterprise* computer—"

He was cut off by loud explosions and ricochet sounds. *Gunshots!* The gunfire was coming from a catwalk far below them, and Picard and Data scurried for cover. When they got out of range, the gunfire stopped, and Data looked curiously at the captain.

Picard shouted, "Hold your fire! We're here to *help* you!"

"Sure you are!" screamed a woman's voice. Another blast of gunfire echoed in the missile silo.

"Captain," said Data, "I believe I can handle this."

Picard nodded, and Data rose to his feet, took a few steps, and jumped off the catwalk. He plummeted twenty meters straight down and landed with a clang on a lower catwalk. The android took another step and leaped again, dropping another twenty meters to the bottom.

The captain heard a woman's scream, and there were several more shots. He could imagine the startled woman emptying her gun at Data with no effect. Picard crawled out from cover, and he could see Data far below, leaning over an unconscious human.

"Captain," called Data, "this woman requires medical attention!"

"We *all* require medical attention," said Beverly Crusher a few minutes later. "She has severe theta-radiation poisoning, and all of us will have to be inoculated for it."

Data studied his tricorder. "The radiation is coming from the damaged throttle assembly."

"I have to get her to Sickbay," said Beverly.

Picard started to protest, but the doctor gave him a stern look. "Jean-Luc, no lectures about the Prime Directive. I'll keep her unconscious."

"Very well," agreed the captain. "Tell Commander Riker to beam down with a search party. We need to find Cochrane."

"Right." Beverly knelt down beside the sick woman, whose dark skin was streaked and sweaty. She tapped her comm badge. "Crusher to *Enterprise.* Two to beam directly to Sickbay." They vanished in a cloud of shimmering lights.

Picard turned to look at Cochrane's damaged ship. "We have less than fourteen hours before this ship has to be launched. We're going to need help."

Geordi La Forge gazed at the humming warp core in the heart of Main Engineering. He didn't know whether it was his newly improved eyesight or the new design, but the warp field *looked* impressive. The entire system pulsed with more power than an antimatter reactor had ever delivered in a Starfleet vessel.

But for some reason it seemed warm in Engineering today. Geordi tugged at his collar to let in some air. He was about to tell Eiger and Porter to investigate the matter when a comm panel beeped.

"Picard to Engineering," came the familiar voice.

"La Forge here, Captain."

"Geordi, Cochrane's ship was damaged in the attack. I want you to assemble an Engineering detail and get down here. We have some work to do."

"Aye, sir." Geordi strode across the room, pointing to members of his staff. "Alpha shift, we're heading down to the surface—assemble in Transporter Room Three. Porter, you're in command here until I get back."

"Aye, sir," answered the young engineer.

Geordi stopped in the doorway and pulled again at his collar. "And take a look at the environmental controls. It's getting a little warm in here."

\* \* \*

Captain Picard stood near the cockpit of the *Phoenix,* watching Geordi and his engineers work far below him. They seemed like Lilliputians crawling all over Gulliver. It wasn't that Cochrane's ship was so large, it just loomed so large in history that Picard couldn't believe they were repairing it.

This flight was the most important event of the twenty-first century, possibly of all time, and they were here to witness it. But where was Zefram Cochrane? History recorded Cochrane making the flight, and it wouldn't do them any good to repair his ship if he couldn't fly it.

Data walked up behind him, and Picard smiled boyishly at him. "Amazing, isn't it? This ship used to be a nuclear missile."

"It is an historical irony that Dr. Cochrane would choose an instrument of mass destruction for his experiment," replied the android.

Picard reached out to touch the famous craft with his hand, feeling the cool metal against his fingers. Data looked puzzledly at him.

"Boyhood fantasy," explained the captain. "I've seen this ship a hundred times in the Smithsonian, but I was never able to touch it."

"Does tactile contact alter your perception of the *Phoenix?*" asked Data.

"Oh, yes. For human beings, the sense of touch is sometimes more important than sight or sound. It connects you to an object, makes it more real."

The android cocked his head at this notion, then he also reached out to touch the ship. He mimicked Picard stroking the hull as the captain waited to see his reaction.

"I can detect imperfections in the titanium casing," said the android, "and temperature variations in the fuel manifold. But it is no more *real* to me now than it was a moment ago."

Counselor Troi strode up to them and stopped. For a few seconds, she watched the captain and Data run their hands over the hull of the warp ship.

"Would you three like to be alone?" she asked.

Picard pulled his hand back with embarrassment, but Data kept stroking the hull as they talked.

"What have you found?" asked the captain.

Troi looked frustrated. "There's no sign of Cochrane anywhere in the complex."

"He must be nearby," insisted Picard. "This experiment meant everything to him. Start searching the community around here. But be careful—the people of this time are desperate and frightened. They're not going to welcome strangers."

"Understood." Troi started off, then stopped. "Captain, we should consider the possibility that Dr. Cochrane was killed in the attack."

"If that's true," said Picard gravely, "then the future may die with him."

In a corridor outside Main Engineering, Paul Porter yanked open a panel over his head. A young woman named Alice Eiger stood nearby, holding a tool kit. Both of them were starting to sweat as they peered into the crawl space above their heads.

"What do you think?" asked Eiger. "What's going on?"

"I have no idea," muttered Porter. "It's like the entire environmental system's gone crazy. And it's not just Engineering—it's this entire deck."

They must have opened up a dozen circuit panels, thought Eiger, but they still hadn't found anything that would account for the heat. "Maybe it's a problem with the EPS conduits," she suggested.

"Or somebody has a sauna in the Jefferies Tube," joked Porter. "Let's check it out." He climbed up the access ladder, through the hatch, and disappeared into the maintenance tube.

Eiger paused to check her tools before starting up the ladder. Suddenly she heard a noise above her, like giant rats running through the woodwork. What the heck was Porter doing?

A head poked out of the hatch, making her jump. But it was just Porter. "Is there anyone else doing maintenance in this section?"

"Not that I know of."

Porter shook his head puzzledly. "I thought I saw somebody. And there's some weird organic cabling around one of the conduits. It doesn't even look like Starfleet technology."

Eiger frowned. "Better get a sample of it."

"Right." Porter disappeared back into the hatch in

the ceiling. A moment later Eiger heard a crunch and a thud above her.

"Paul?" she asked with concern.

There was no response.

"You okay up there?"

Once again, there was no response, and Eiger made her way slowly up the ladder.

# CHAPTER 4

In the missile silo, Captain Picard watched the engineers unload another batch of spare parts. Replicators were working overtime on the *Enterprise* to create parts identical to the ones that Cochrane had used on his ship. It had to be all twenty-first-century technology.

Luckily, the *Phoenix* was so famous that the blueprints were standard study materials. From computer records they could duplicate parts, but could they get the ship flying in time?

Picard leaned over the railing of the catwalk to watch the team working on the intercooling system. Suddenly the eerie voices of the Borg invaded his mind, and he bolted upright. He held his breath until the babble of voices faded away.

Deanna Troi looked at him with concern. "Captain, what is it?"

He frowned. "I'm not sure." A moment later he tapped his comm badge. "Picard to *Enterprise*. Is everything all right up there, Mr. Worf?"

"Yes, sir," said the deep-voiced Klingon. "We are experiencing some environmental difficulties on Deck Sixteen, but that is all."

"What kind of difficulties?" asked Picard with a feeling of dread.

"Humidity levels have risen by seventy-two percent, and the temperature has jumped ten degrees in the last hour."

"Data and I are returning to the ship," said the captain.

"Understood."

Picard shouted down to Riker, "Number One, take charge down here."

"Aye, sir!" came the response.

"I'm needed on the ship," said the captain, more to himself than anyone else.

Beverly Crusher gazed at the newest patient in Sickbay, a woman from Earth's past. Humans hadn't changed much in three hundred years, thought the doctor. If you cleaned the woman up and put her in a uniform, she could pass for a member of the crew.

With a surgical sponge, Beverly wiped the sweat from her brow, wondering if this heat would ever let up. Her entire staff was suffering from the unusual heat and humidity.

She lifted the clamshell diagnostic device off the patient's chest and checked the readouts. Her assistant, Nurse Alyssa Ogawa, came to her side.

"I've repaired the damage to her cell membranes," said Beverly. "But I'd like to run some tests on her spinal tissues. Any idea why it's so *hot* in here?"

Ogawa shook her head. "We can't turn it down."

Suddenly the lights flickered and went out, and every panel and terminal in the room went dead. In the dying phosphors of light, Beverly could see only vague shapes around her.

"Now what?" muttered Beverly. She tapped her comm badge. "Crusher to Engineering."

There was no answer. She tried again. "Crusher to Bridge."

Again there was no answer, at least not from the communication device. From all around them in the darkness came strange skittering noises, as if the walls were filled with giant rats. Beverly grabbed a tricorder and scanned the walls. It only took a few seconds to find out what it was:

*The Borg!*

Captain Picard and Data strode onto the bridge only to find a sorry collection of worried looks. Even Worf appeared glum.

"Report," barked the captain.

Worf scowled. "We have just lost contact with Deck Sixteen—communications, internal sensors, everything. I was about to send a security team to investigate."

"No," snapped Picard. "Seal off Deck Sixteen and post security teams at every access point." He tried not to think about the people down there.

As Worf entered the commands on his tactical console, Picard strode behind Lieutenant Hawk on the Conn. "Mr. Hawk, before we lost internal sensors, what were the exact environmental conditions in Main Engineering?"

Hawk checked his console. "Atmospheric pressure was ten kilopascals above normal. Ninety-two percent humidity, and—"

"Thirty-nine-point-one degrees Celsius," said Picard, finishing Hawk's sentence.

"Yes, sir." Hawk blinked at him.

"The same as a Borg ship," said Picard.

Nobody moved on the bridge of the *Enterprise,* as the meaning of Picard's statement sunk in.

"Borg?" asked Worf. "On the *Enterprise?*"

The captain nodded grimly. "They realized their ship was doomed, so they beamed over during the battle, while our shields were down. First they assimilate the *Enterprise*—then Earth."

He hit the comm panel. "Picard to Commander Riker." The only answer was increased static. *"Enterprise* to away team—respond!"

At that moment the lights on the bridge began to flicker, and consoles started going dark one after another.

"Sir!" shouted Hawk, "command control is being rerouted to Main Engineering! Weapons, shields, propulsion—"

"Data," ordered Picard, "quickly—lock out the main computer!"

The android rushed to a console, and his fingers were a blur as they worked the controls. Within seconds, he was finished.

"I have isolated the main computer with a fractal encryption code," explained Data. "It is highly unlikely the Borg will be able to break it."

More lights went out, leaving only a few consoles still operating. "The Borg have cut power to all decks," reported Worf, "except Sixteen."

"But without the computer," said Hawk, "they won't be able to control the ship."

"The Borg won't stay on Deck Sixteen," said Picard with certainty.

"Wake up!" shouted Beverly Crusher, rudely shaking her newest patient. This wasn't the time for nice bedside manners. "We have to *move* it! Wake up!"

From outside the main doors and access panels, the Borg were trying to smash their way into Sickbay. Attendants hustled their patients out the Jefferies Tubes as quickly as possible, but it wasn't quick enough.

Lily Sloane opened her eyes drowsily and stared at Beverly. "Where . . . what?"

"There's no time to explain," snapped Beverly. "I need you to sit up."

Lily tried to stand up, but she was just coming out of sedation. As she started to fall, Nurse Ogawa steadied her.

"Alyssa, take her and go!" ordered Beverly.

Ogawa grabbed the confused woman and ushered her toward the Jefferies Tube. "Those doors won't hold much longer!"

"We need a diversion," said Beverly. "Is the EMH still on?"

"It should be. The holo-buffers are still functioning." Ogawa steered her patient toward the Jefferies Tube.

Terrible pounding came on the main door, and the panels started to buckle inward.

"I swore I'd never use one of those things," muttered Beverly. "Computer! Activate the EMH program."

A holographic doctor appeared out of thin air. He was the same sardonic balding doctor that many Starfleet crews had come to know.

"Please state the nature of the medical emergency," he said with a superior air.

"Twenty Borg are about to break down that door," answered Beverly, "and we need time to get out of here. Create a diversion!"

"This isn't part of my program," complained the hologram. "I'm a doctor, not a doorstop."

"Dance for them, tell a story—I don't care! Just give us a few extra seconds." Beverly rushed for the Jefferies Tube and hurried the last of her staff up the ladder.

Just as the main doors of Sickbay blew open, she hurried up the ladder and into the steamy darkness of the Jefferies Tube. If the doctor didn't do *something,* they would be on her tail in an instant.

As Beverly crawled away, she could hear the Borg tromp into Sickbay. Then she heard the holograph's voice:

"According to Starfleet medical research," he said, "Borg implants cause severe skin irritations. Perhaps you'd like an . . . analgesic cream?"

Crawling like mad, Beverly rounded a corner in the crawl space and ran into her patient, the woman from the past. Nurse Ogawa and the others were also slowing down.

"Which way?" asked Ogawa.

Beverly squeezed past the rest of them in the narrow space and led them into a side tunnel. "Follow me. We need to get off this deck!"

Thinking that everyone was following her, the doctor plowed ahead. She didn't see her patient take off in the opposite direction.

Ten Starfleet security officers grabbed phaser rifles out of the weapons locker and stood at attention. Picard, Worf, and Data strode through the command post, inspecting the security detail.

"The first thing they'll do in Engineering," said Picard, "is establish a Collective—a central point from where they'll control the hive."

He activated a screen on the wall to show them a schematic of Main Engineering. "The problem is, if we begin firing particle weapons inside Engineering, we risk hitting the warp core. So I believe our goal should be to puncture one of the plasma coolant tanks."

Picard adjusted the image to show the coolant tanks. They blinked with biohazard symbols. "What do you think, Data?"

"An excellent plan," agreed the android. "Plasma coolant will liquefy any organic material on contact."

"But the Borg aren't entirely organic," warned Worf.

"No," said Picard, "but they can't survive without their organic components."

Worf hefted his phaser rifle. "I have ordered all weapons to be set on a rotating modulation. But the Borg will adapt quickly. We will have a dozen shots at most."

"One other thing," said Picard grimly. "Warn your teams they may encounter *Enterprise* crew members who have already been assimilated. They mustn't hesitate to fire. Believe me, you'll be doing them a favor."

The captain grabbed a phaser rifle and shouldered his way past the security detail. "Let's go."

# CHAPTER

# 5

As the *Enterprise* orbited the unsuspecting planet, Picard, Data, and a team of five security officers jogged down a darkened corridor. With their phaser rifles and grim sweaty faces, they looked prepared for anything.

By a different route, Worf was also leading a team to Engineering. The thinking was that if one team couldn't get through, perhaps the other one could. If both teams made it to the rendezvous, even better. Both teams were also to look for survivors along the way.

The captain didn't want to think about what might have happened to Beverly and her staff, or the people in Engineering. He tried to put his emotions out of his mind—along with those awful voices.

Data stopped in front of a bulkhead, reached down, and pulled up a deck plate. Underneath it was a large hatch that dropped into total darkness. Picard took the lead and jumped down feetfirst.

With a thud, the captain landed on the deck below him and dropped into a crouch. It was so dark that he had to activate the lightbeam on his phaser rifle. The captain shined the light around but saw no movement, so he motioned to Data above him. He sunk back against the bulkhead as the rest of the team dropped down.

A moment later they were running down another dark corridor, with only the lights from their rifles to guide them. At an intersection, an open access panel caught Picard's eyes, and he stopped to investigate. He gulped when he got a good look:

Dark pulsing Borg technology lay choking the old Starfleet circuits. Partially organic, the strange machines flowed with murky liquids and made eerie clicking and sucking sounds. Picard shined his light down the corridor—the entire length of it was covered with Borg machinery!

Even Data looked worried. "Captain," said the android, "I believe I am feeling . . . anxiety. It is an intriguing sensation. I can see how it would be distracting."

Picard scowled. "I'm sure it's a fascinating experience, but perhaps you should deactivate your emotion chip for now."

"Good idea, sir." Data tilted his head, and all traces of nervousness left his face. "Done."

"Data, there are times I envy you," said Picard. "Come on."

The captain cautiously led his team down a corridor covered with alien growth. As they rounded a corner, two Borg marched right past them. The security team leveled their phaser rifles, but Picard raised his hand to stop them.

"Hold your fire," he said. "They'll ignore us—until they consider us a threat."

The two Borg walked right past the humans without even looking at them. Picard motioned his team to follow them, and they trailed the Borg until they were about twenty meters away from double doors marked MAIN ENGINEERING.

In this part of the ship, every centimeter of the *Enterprise* had been taken over by the Borg machines. Boxes lined the corridors, and each box contained a sleeping Borg. To Picard, it felt as if he were reliving his nightmare all over again. But this was real!

Worse yet, some of the boxes contained Borg who had been his officers only a few hours earlier. They were adding to their number by assimilating crew members.

"Captain," said Data.

Picard whirled around to see Worf coming from the other direction with his team. He was glad to see the big Klingon, and he signaled for them to merge their teams. They had come this far easily, but the rest of their mission wouldn't be so easy.

"We found Dr. Crusher and her staff," said Worf. "They escaped by a Jefferies Tube."

Picard let out a sigh. "Good. We have to get inside Engineering and put a stop to this."

With Picard and Data in the lead, the united team walked toward the doors leading to Engineering. Worf and his security officers spread out around them protectively, their phasers leveled and ready. It was a long and tense walk, passing by so many sleeping Borg.

They didn't seem to be aware of the security team, but Picard knew that wasn't true. They would respond as soon as the intruders did something to endanger the Collective. If his team was lucky, they could break the Borg's grip on Engineering before they awoke.

The team approached the main doors, which were covered in black thickets of Borg machinery. The doors didn't open automatically, which was no surprise. They would have to override the Borg machinery. Behind a clump of Borg circuits was an access panel, and Picard nodded to Data.

With a steady hand, Data reached out for the access panel. His fingers closed around the emergency release handle, and the android looked again at Picard. The captain glanced at Worf and the security team, and they leveled their weapons, ready for action. Picard nodded, and Data pulled on the handle.

With a crack, it broke off in his hand. Data looked puzzledly at Picard.

"Perhaps we should just knock," said the captain with a slight smile.

Suddenly a chorus of clicking and whirring sounds

greeted their ears, and they whirled around to see boxes moving. The Borg were coming out of their sleep. Slowly the cyborgs detached themselves from their energy sources and stepped out of their alcoves. There were dozens of them, down the entire length of the corridor.

Stiffly and silently, the Borg began to walk toward them. They lifted their arms, revealing deadly drills, probes, and needlelike instruments. Picard looked around desperately. With a locked door at their backs, there was no escape except *through* the Borg.

"Ready phasers," ordered Worf tensely. The security officers wasted no time in obeying. The stone-faced Borg kept coming closer and closer. Worf waited until they were well in range, then he barked, "Fire!"

The first row of security officers fired their phasers, hitting two of the Borg squarely in their chests. With blue sparks shooting from their bodies, the Borg slumped to the deck, but other Borg stepped over them and kept coming.

Worf's team kept firing, and two more cyborgs were blasted backward. But the rest kept advancing— unstoppable, uncaring. Data stepped in front of Picard to protect him, and the captain knew that they were in trouble.

He yanked open the access panel and began ripping out the Borg circuits as fast as he could. He had to get that door open!

Behind him the battle raged, as Worf and his team kept firing away. So many Borg fell that their bodies piled up in the corridor, but more kept stepping over them. Worf shot one in the center of his chest, but the beam hit a shield and bounced off.

"Captain!" shouted Worf. "They've adapted!"

Picard turned back to the access panel. He plugged in wires that the Borg had disconnected, and the doors jerked open a few centimeters. The captain could see nothing but darkness inside the engineering room, but it was their only escape.

He rushed to the doors and tried to pull them apart. Groaning with the effort, he finally pushed the doors open wide enough to wedge his body inside. He thought they were going to escape, until a Borg leaped out of Engineering and knocked him down.

Picard struggled with his foe, but the Borg tried to push a drill into his face. The captain grabbed it with both hands. He struggled with all his might, but he wasn't strong enough to fight a Borg by himself.

Suddenly Data stepped in, grabbed the cyborg, and hurled him into a bulkhead. But three more Borg rushed out of Engineering and grabbed Data.

"Captain!" called the android, as the Borg dragged him into Engineering.

Picard tried to help his friend, but the Borg dragged him swiftly into the darkness of Engineering. The doors clanged shut behind them.

The captain had no time to worry about Data, because dozens of Borg were moving down the hallway, surrounding them. Their phasers rifles were ineffective, so the security officers were using them as clubs. But it was no use.

A Borg grabbed one of the security men and injected something into his neck. The man's eyes went blank, and tiny machines began to crawl under his skin.

"Regroup on Deck Fifteen!" shouted Picard. "Don't let them touch you!"

In the mad scramble that followed, it was every man for himself. The captain ran through the Borg drones like a football player breaking through the line. With his own survival in doubt, he couldn't help anyone else.

Finally he found a ladder and began climbing into a Jefferies Tube. He heard Worf shouting to his team, leading them off in another direction. But Borg were swarming all around, and Picard couldn't wait to see what happened next. As they reached for his legs, he bounded upward into the dark tube.

Picard scrambled through the crawl space for several minutes, and it got darker and darker. He was beginning to think that he had escaped, when a tendril whipped out and wrapped around his neck!

He was sure it was a Borg! Instinctively he dropped his phaser and threw his body into his foe, smashing him against the wall. At once, the tendril around his neck loosened, and he realized it was an optical cable. He whirled to face his opponent and saw it was not a Borg.

It was a wild-eyed woman with torn dirty clothes— the same woman they had rescued from the silo. Only now she was holding his phaser.

"You!" he said in amazement. "How did you—"

"Back off," she warned Picard, leveling his own

phaser at him. There was fear in her eyes, but also determination.

"Calm down," he said slowly.

"Shut up," she said, snarling. "Who *are* you?"

"My name is Jean—"

"No, who are you with? What *faction?*"

There were strange shuffling noises nearby, and Picard wanted to keep moving. "I'm not part of the Eastern Coalition," he said. "Look, this is difficult to explain, but—"

"I said, shut up! I don't care *who* you're with, just get me out of this . . . whatever this place is."

"That's not going to be easy."

"Well, you'd better find a way to make it easy, or I'm going to start pressing buttons." Lily leveled his phaser at him.

Putting distance between them and the Borg sounded like a good idea to Picard. "Follow me."

As the captain made his way down the Jefferies Tube, he tried not to think about the phaser at his back.

# CHAPTER

# 6

Data opened his eyes to find himself strapped to a table, hanging upside down in the engineering room. Actually, thought the android, it would be more accurate to call it the Borg hive. Except for the warp core and a few consoles, the entire room had been converted to Borg equipment.

The room had a moist organic feel to it, with various dripping and chirping sounds. Boxes lined the walls from deck to ceiling, and each contained a Borg. Other Borg moved silently around the hive, attending to the ones who were sleeping.

The table suddenly rotated and lowered itself to the deck. Even though he knew he was in grave danger, the android couldn't help but be curious. As the table descended he looked all around the hive.

In one corner, four Borg were attached to a series of hoses dangling from the ceiling. In fact, the entire ceiling was filled with dark dripping hoses and conduits. Murky liquids flowed in and out of the cyborgs' bodies, as if they were feeding.

He looked around and could see other Borg working at Engineering consoles. From the data flashing across their screens, he could tell what they were trying to do.

"Your efforts to break the encryption codes will not be successful," he told them. "Nor will your attempts to assimilate me into your Collective."

"Brave words," said a sultry woman's voice. "I've heard them before from thousands of species across thousands of worlds . . . long before you were created."

Data followed the sound of the voice and looked up to the ceiling. There was a rustle of movement in the tangle of hoses and machinery, and something began to descend. It was like a snake slithering out of the weeds, and Data craned his neck to see it.

A face! There was a woman's face in the sea of hoses and conduits. She was pale-skinned, with raven hair and piercing eyes. She was unlike any Borg that Data had ever seen. Then she rose back into the ceiling and vanished.

"Now all of them are Borg," said the sultry voice.

Three Borg moved toward Data, armed with drills and probes. He tried to ignore them.

"I am unlike any life-form you have encountered

before," said Data. "The codes stored in my neural net cannot be forcibly removed."

"You are an imperfect being," replied the woman, "created by an imperfect being. Finding your weakness is only a matter of time."

The Borg hovered closer with their drills and probes. Data twitched as they began to drill into his head, then everything went blank.

Night had fallen on the missile complex in Montana, and the survivors of the Borg attack were putting their town back together. Some picked up debris, while others rebuilt the shacks. Much of their primitive equipment was wrecked, but the jukebox in the Crash and Burn was working again.

These were resilient people, thought Will Riker. He admired them, except he had doubts about the great hero of the twenty-first century, Zefram Cochrane. Deanna had found him in a bar, drunk, and now they were trying to explain to him what was happening. It wasn't easy.

Geordi had set up a crude twenty-first-century telescope, and he was checking the angle with his tricorder. While he prepared his experiment, Troi and Riker watched Cochrane.

"Are you ready to listen?" asked Riker.

The scientist rubbed his eyes. "I've been listening. You're some kind of 'commander,' and a group of cybernetic aliens from the future have traveled back through time to enslave the human race. And you're here to stop them."

Riker nodded, pleased. "That's right."

"God, you're heroic. Can you fly, too?"

Riker scowled. "We're going to prove it to you." He turned to look at the telescope. "Geordi, how are you doing?"

"These old refractors are tricky to align, but I think I've got it." Geordi peered into the eyepiece. "Yeah, come take a look."

Riker looked expectantly at Cochrane, and the doctor finally scowled and stood up. He shuffled over to the telescope. "What do we have here? I love a good peep show . . ." His voice trailed off as he looked into the eyepiece.

"It's a trick," he snapped. "How'd you do that?"

"It's *your* telescope," said Geordi.

Cochrane frowned and looked again. "Yes, there is a weird ship up there in orbit. But I still don't believe it."

"Believe it," said Riker. "That's our ship—the *Enterprise.*"

"And Lily's up there right now?" asked Cochrane in amazement. "Can I talk to her?"

Riker shook his head. "We've lost contact with the *Enterprise.* We don't know why."

Cochrane looked at them with a worried expression. "So . . . what is it you want me to do?"

"Simple," answered Riker. "Go on your warp flight, just as you planned."

"Well, all right," said Cochrane doubtfully. "But it'll take a couple of weeks to build a new field generator—"

"We have the technology to repair your ship to-night," said Geordi.

When Cochrane stared at them, Riker added, "It's imperative that you make the flight tomorrow morning, by eleven fifteen at the latest."

"Why?" asked Cochrane.

"Because at eleven o'clock, an alien ship will be passing through this solar system."

The scientist frowned again, as if this was all too much to think about. "More bad guys?"

"Good guys," said Troi. "They're on a survey mission. They have no interest in Earth . . . too primitive."

"But tomorrow morning," added Riker, "when they detect the warp signature from your ship, they'll realize that humans have discovered how to travel faster than the speed of light. They'll decide to alter course, and make First Contact with Earth . . . right here."

"Here?" asked Cochrane, looking around at the bombed-out town.

Geordi pointed toward the silo. "Right over there. I think that's where the monument's going to be. It's one of the most pivotal moments in human history, Doctor. You get to make First Contact with an alien race. And after you do, everything begins to change."

"It unites people in a way that no one thought possible," said Troi, "once they realize they're not alone in the universe."

Excitedly, Geordi went on, "Your theories on warp drive allow fleets of starships to be built. And humans start exploring the galaxy. Eventually, Earth and a handful of other worlds form an interstellar government called the United Federation of Planets."

"And before long," said Deanna, "Earth becomes a paradise. Poverty, disease, war—they'll all be gone from this planet in the next fifty years."

"But," warned Riker, "unless you make that warp flight tomorrow before eleven fifteen, none of it will happen."

Cochrane just stared at them. "And you people . . . you're all astronauts on some kind of . . . star trek?"

Geordi smiled. "I know this has been a lot for you to take in, Doc. But we're running out of time. We need your help. Are you with us?"

Cochrane looked doubtful, but he managed a weak smile. "Why not?"


On the *Enterprise,* Picard and Lily made their way slowly down a corridor, past rows of Borg drones sleeping in their compartments. The walls and ceiling were covered with Borg machinery and tubes.

If that wasn't bad enough, a confused woman from the past held a phaser on Picard, thinking he was the enemy.

"Why'd you break the cease-fire?" she demanded.

"We're not the ones who attacked you—"

"Who did?"

Picard finally spotted the umbilical docking port, which looked like a small room that sloped outward at a forty-five-degree angle. He stopped, wondering if it wouldn't be better to give her her wish. If they couldn't get the Borg under control, *all* of them might have to abandon ship.

"There's a new faction that wants to prevent your launch tomorrow," he lied. "But we're here to help you."

"You want to help?" she asked doubtfully. "Get me out of here."

There was no avoiding for long, decided Picard. "This might be difficult for you to accept, but you're not on Earth anymore. You're in a spaceship, orbiting at an altitude of about two hundred and fifty thousand kilometers."

She pointed the phaser right at his nose. "I think it's time to press the red one. What do you think?"

"All right, you want a way out? Here it is!" Picard tapped a control panel, and the wall slid open, revealing a huge circular portal that was open to space. Below them was Earth, shimmering like a giant blue marble.

The stunned look on Lily's face was priceless. She stared down at the planet and grabbed a ridge in the bulkhead, as if worried about falling out.

"What? What is this?" She gasped.

Picard pointed out some landmarks. "That's Australia . . . New Guinea . . . Montana should be coming up soon. But you might want to hold your breath, it's a long way down."

When tears welled up in the woman's eyes, he

realized that this was a sight she couldn't possibly see in her world. He looked at her sympathetically. "Listen to me, I'm not your enemy. I can get you home, but you'll have to put that weapon down . . . and trust me."

The woman looked at him doubtfully. She didn't want to hand the weapon over, but she couldn't ignore what she had seen with her own eyes. If she was going to get out of this alive, she would need his help.

"My name is Jean-Luc Picard," he said pleasantly. "What's yours?"

"Lily."

"Welcome aboard, Lily." He held out his hand, and she finally handed him the phaser.

"Thank you." Picard glanced at the setting and smiled.

"What?" she asked.

"It was only set to level one. If you had shot me, it would've given me a rather nasty rash."

"Hey," she answered, "it was my first ray gun."

They smiled at each other, and the tension between them began to ease. Then she stared out the port again, fascinated.

"There's no glass," she said with amazement.

Picard reached into the invisible barrier, which sizzled at his touch. "Forcefield."

"I've never seen that kind of technology," said Lily.

"That's because it has not been invented yet."

Captain Picard (Patrick Stewart) is haunted by nightmares of himself as Locutus of Borg.

Lieutenant Commander Worf (Michael Dorn) commands the *Defiant* during Starfleet's unsuccessful attempt to stop the Borg.

Lieutenant Commander La Forge (LeVar Burton) wonders what could be causing the temperature to rise in engineering.

Unfazed by the Borg's transformation of the lower decks of the *Enterprise,* Worf's security detail heads for engineering.

Deanna Troi (Marina Sirtis) and Will Riker (Jonathan Frakes)
must convince Zefram Cochrane of the importance of his flight.

Dr. Cochrane (James Cromwell) does not believe the officers
of the *Enterprise*.

The Borg have captured and transformed engineering into a lair of their Collective.

Determined to stop the Borg, Dr. Crusher (Gates McFadden), Lieutenant Hawk (Neal McDonough), and Lieutenant Commander Worf take aim.

Clinging to the exterior of the ship, Worf draws his *mek'leth* and kills the attacker.

Captain Picard (Patrick Stewart) is determined to draw the line here and now and stop the Borg.

When other methods fail, Riker chooses a new means of persuasion to halt Cochrane's escape.

Cochrane breaks the warp barrier as before—but with some additional help.

The Borg Queen (Alice Krige) does not comprehend Data's drive to become human.

Data (Brent Spiner) is captured by the Borg, who seek his knowledge of encrypting codes for the main computer.

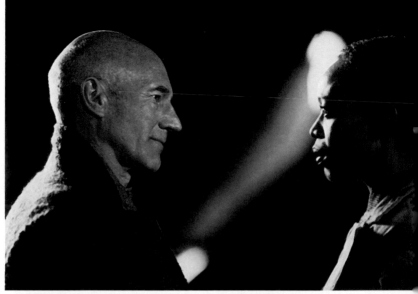
Picard bids Lily (Alfre Woodard) a fond farewell.

Having made its first tentative step to the stars, humanity plays host to its first official off-world visitors, the Vulcans.

Riker," he said, "there's a humanoid five hundred meters ahead of us."

Riker stopped. "Cochrane?"

Geordi stared into the distance with his digitized vision and zoomed in on a thermal signature. He could see the swirling patterns of heat as a man ran through the woods. The man stopped, took something out of his pocket, and took a drink.

"It's him, all right," said Geordi.

Riker motioned to the others. "Wait here. Geordi and I will handle it."

The two of them made their way slowly through the trees to a spot where Cochrane sat on a rock, breathing heavily. He didn't see them until they were almost on top of him. When he tried to run in one direction, Geordi cut him off. When he tried to run in the other direction, Riker cut him off.

"Still looking for the bathroom?" asked Geordi.

"I'm not going back!" shouted Cochrane.

"Doc, we can't do this without you," insisted Geordi.

"I don't care! I don't *want* a statue!"

Riker took a step toward him, and Cochrane took a swing at him. "Get away from me!"

"We don't have time for this," growled Riker. He drew his phaser pistol, aimed, and fired at Cochrane. Stunned, the scientist dropped into the leaves on the forest floor.

Riker turned to Geordi and shook his head. "You told him about the *statue?*"

\* \* \*

Picard started to hear the scraping noises again. "There's something else I have to tell you, but let's do it as we walk—"

In the Borg hive, which had once been Main Engineering, Data was still strapped to the operating table. He was alert again, and he found that his arm and shoulder were encased in some kind of Borg shell. Tubes were pumping liquid in and out of his body.

Two Borg stood nearby, awaiting orders. Something was about to happen; Data could sense it.

He heard the voice of the mysterious woman. "Are you ready?"

Data stared at the tangle of hoses and conduits in the ceiling. "Who are you?"

"I am the Borg."

"That is a contradiction," said Data. "The Borg act as a collective consciousness. There are no individuals."

Out of the darkness at the top of the hive, the head and upper shoulders of a woman began to descend. She had dark hair, pale skin, and cold silvery eyes. Her spine was made of Borg machinery. She was like a queen, thought Data—a Borg Queen.

Like a snake dropping from a tree, she moved slowly toward Data. A web of tubes and machinery stretched with her. In a low voice, she said, "I am the beginning . . . the end . . . the one who is many. I am the Borg."

Her head and shoulders descended into a synthetic

Borg body, and the tubes broke off and flew away. The Queen walked toward him on her mechanical legs, swinging her mechanical arms.

"Greetings," said Data politely. "I am curious. Do you control the Borg Collective?"

"You imply a disparity where none exists. I *am* the Collective."

"Perhaps I should rephrase the question," said Data. "I wish to understand the organizational relationships. Are you their leader?"

"I bring order to chaos."

"An interesting, if cryptic, response."

The Borg Queen looked at him disdainfully. "You are in chaos, Data. You are the contradiction—a machine who wishes to be human."

"There is no contradiction. I simply wish to evolve . . . to better myself. That is a drive common to many species."

"We, too, are on a quest to better ourselves," said the Borg. "We are evolving toward a state of perfection."

"Forgive me," said Data, "but you do not evolve—you conquer."

The Borg Queen smiled at him. "By assimilating other beings into our Collective, we are bringing them closer to perfection as well."

"Somehow I question your motives," said Data.

"That's because you haven't been properly stimulated yet." The way the Queen was looking at him made Data very anxious.

"You have reactivated my emotion chip. Why?"

"Don't be frightened."

"I am not frightened," said Data, although he wasn't sure that statement was entirely truthful.

But the Queen didn't respond. Instead she looked intently at the casing on his arm and shoulder. It popped open at her silent command.

Data lifted his head to see what had been done to his arm. His artificial skin had been stripped away to show the servos and circuits underneath. But growing on his forearm was something new and strange—a small patch of real skin! It was held in place by hooks, clamps, and tubes, but it appeared real.

"Do you know what this is, Data?" asked the Borg Queen.

"It would appear you are attempting to graft organic skin onto my endoskeletal structure."

"What a cold description for such a beautiful gift." The Queen bent over his body until her lips were only a few centimeters from his new skin. She blew softly on it, and he could *feel* the goose bumps rising. It was the most human sensation he had ever felt!

"Was that good for you?" asked the Queen, making Data more frightened and confused than ever.

He didn't want to admit it, but it *was* good for him.

# CHAPTER

## 7

Captain Picard and Lily finally reached a corridor that hadn't been taken over by the Borg yet. Picard went instantly to an active computer console and tried to enter some commands.

"How many planets are in this . . . Federation?" asked Lily.

"Over one hundred fifty, spread across eight thousand light years."

"You must not get home much," said Lily with a sympathetic smile.

The captain shrugged. "Actually I tend to think of this ship as home. But if it's Earth you're talking about, I do try to get back when I can."

For the third straight time, Picard got a message

from the panel reading ACCESS DENIED. That was fine with him, because it meant that the Borg were still locked out, too.

"Good," he said. "They haven't broken the encryption codes yet."

"Who? Those bionic zombies you told me about? The—"

"Borg." Picard scowled.

"Oh, yeah, right. Sounds Swedish."

"So how big is this ship?" asked Lily.

"Twenty-four decks, almost seven hundred meters long."

She shook her head. "It took me six months to scrounge up enough titanium just to build a four-meter cockpit. How much did this thing cost?"

The captain smiled. "The economics of the future are somewhat different. Money doesn't exist in the twenty-fourth century.

"No money? You don't get *paid?"*

"Wealth is no longer a driving force in our lives. We work to better ourselves and the rest of humanity. We're actually quite like *you* and Dr. Cochrane."

To his surprise, Lily burst out laughing.

"What?" asked Picard, following her around the corner.

Both of them stopped short at the sight of a corridor lined with whirring gurgling Borg equipment. There were a dozen Borg lining the walls in their boxes and several more working. Trying to get away, Lily turned and bumped into Picard.

He grabbed her shoulders and tried to calm her. "It's all right. They won't attack us unless we threaten them. Come on."

Gently, Picard steered her into the corridor, hoping they could sneak through without alerting the cyborgs. A Borg suddenly jolted out of its box and swerved toward Lily. She ducked down, expecting to be attacked, but the Borg walked right past her.

The captain took her hand and led her a little farther down the grotesque corridor. Then the voices came—shuddering, murmuring, working their way into his brain. They wanted him to join them, and some part of him was still paying attention.

"Definitely not Swedish," said Lily in a shaky voice.

All around him, the Borg were working in the access panel, converting this deck to their use. If he didn't stop them, the newest *Enterprise* would soon be a Borg ship. In this century, that would be disastrous. Picard looked around and realized that the holodeck was on this level. Then he lifted his phaser and fired!

The blue beam caught one of the Borg in the chest, and he exploded in a splash of blood and metal. Two of the Borg turned and marched toward them, ready to deal with this new threat.

"What did you do that for?" wailed Lily.

Picard grabbed her hand and ran down the corridor, with the two Borg in pursuit. They stopped outside the doors that led to the holodeck, and Picard hit the control panel. To his relief, the doors whooshed open.

He dragged Lily inside a huge room with a black grid on the floor, walls, and ceiling. There was nothing else in the room except for a glowing computer panel.

"Is there another way out of here!" asked Lily with alarm.

Picard rushed to the computer panel and turned it on. He quickly entered the name of a program, then turned to look at Lily. "Perhaps something in satin—"

She gave him a puzzled look, then the Borg began beating on the doors, trying to force them open. The metal groaned as they banged the doors back and stepped into the holodeck.

Only it wasn't a holodeck any longer but a long foyer in a swanky nightclub. Two people vanished at the far end of the hallway, but there were more people hanging around. They were dressed in shiny tuxedos and slinky evening gowns from the 1930s. For a few seconds the Borg didn't know what to do.

Picard dragged Lily into the nightclub, which was as big as a ballroom. On stage the dance band was packing up their instruments, getting ready to go home for the night. There were only a few people left, sitting around, chatting and drinking.

Picard was wearing the fedora hat and trench-coat he usually wore when he was pretending to be

Dixon Hill, a private detective. Lily was dressed in a shimmering satin evening gown. She just stared blankly at him as he dragged her through this bizarre place.

Picard spotted a friend behind the bar and called, "Eddie!"

The bartender looked up from the glasses he was washing. "Dixon!"

Suddenly a drunken man bumped into Lily. "Hey, Beautiful," he slurred, "wanna dance?"

Picard stared at the man. "She's with me." The man backed off, and they kept moving.

"I thought you said none of this was real?" asked Lily puzzledly.

"It's not. They're all holograms."

"That guy sure *felt* real."

Picard heard voices, and he looked back to see the two Borg in the doorway of the nightclub. A *maître d'* in a tuxedo walked up and gave them a fishy look.

"I'm sorry, gentlemen," he said, "but we're closing."

"And you do understand, we have a strict dress code. So if you boys don't leave right now, I'll—"

One of the Borg grabbed the host by the collar and lifted him into the air. A laser probe shot from the Borg's eyepiece and hit the maître d', who turned invisible for a second. The Borg threw him aside, and both of them marched into the nightclub.

Picard turned to the bartender, who gave him a smile. "What'll it be, Dix? The usual?"

"I'm looking for Nicky the Nose," said Picard, remembering the worst of a bad lot.

"The Nose?" asked the bartender. "He ain't been in here for months."

"Oh, no," said Picard, "this is the wrong chapter." Loudly he said, "Computer, begin chapter thirteen."

Lily's eyes widened as everyone in the nightclub turned into different people, on a different night. The band was playing, and dozens of couples were dancing, eating, drinking. There were a lot more people.

But two things were the same—the Borg who were moving through the nightclub, inspecting everyone.

Picard swept Lily out onto the dance floor, and they began to fox-trot. "Try to look like you're having a good time," suggested Picard. Lily glanced worriedly at the Borg.

"No, look at me," he ordered. "Try to act naturally."

She managed a strained smile. "Come here often?" Picard guided her slowly away from the Borg. "You're not a bad dancer," she added.

He spotted Nicky the Nose in a corner booth, sitting with one of his henchmen. Nick was a fat mobster with a metal nose—someone had bitten it off years ago. Picard guided Lily toward the gangsters.

Suddenly someone grabbed him, turned him around, and kissed him. He looked up to see Ruby, a gorgeous friend of Dixon Hill's. She gave Lily a suspicious look.

"Ruby," said Picard with embarrassment, "this isn't really a good time."

The woman frowned. "It's never the time for us, is it, Dix? Always some excuse . . . some case you're working on."

"Yeah, I gotta talk to Nicky. I'll see you later on."

"Okay, but watch your caboose. And dump the broad." With a catty look at Lily, Ruby sauntered off.

Picard finally made it to the booth where Nicky the Nose and his henchman were sitting.

"What's shakin', Dix?" asked the Nose.

"Just the usual, Nick. Martinis and skirts." Picard ran his hands over the henchman's chest, looking for a gun.

"Hey," growled the henchman, "I'm gonna take this personal in a second."

He had no gun! Picard turned to see the Borg, who were knocking people out of their way as they crossed the room. Picard finally spotted a violin case on the floor, only he knew it didn't contain a violin.

He reached for the violin case, and the henchman tried to stop him. But Lily hit the man over the head with a champagne bucket; he fell to the floor in a shower of ice cubes.

With the Borg nearly on top of him, Picard popped open the violin case and whipped out an old-fashioned Tommy gun. The patrons in the club screamed and ran for cover as he whirled to face the Borg.

Picard cut loose with a hail of bullets. Glasses and

bottles shattered everywhere, and the first Borg spun around and smashed through a table. The second one kept coming, and Picard kept firing with grim determination. Finally both Borg lay on the floor, twitching, with sparks shooting out of their bodies.

As the smoke cleared, he walked over and stared at the Borg. Lily walked up behind him. "I think you got 'em," she said dryly.

Picard leaned over one of the dead Borg and opened a panel on his stomach.

"I don't get it," said Lily. "You said this was all a bunch of holograms. If the gun isn't real—"

"I disengaged the safety protocols," answered Picard. "Without them, even a holographic bullet can kill." He reached deep inside the alien circuitry.

"What are you doing?" asked Lily.

"Looking for the neuroprocessor. Every Borg has one. It's like a memory chip—it'll contain a record of the instructions this Borg's been receiving from the Collective."

Picard cleared his throat and went back to work on the Borg. Lily leaned over his shoulder and pointed to the red material across the Borg's chest.

"Hey, that's one of your uniforms," she said with surprise.

Picard nodded grimly. "This was Ensign Lynch."

With relief, he found what he was looking for, and he pulled a chunk of circuitry from the dead Borg. Carefully, Picard removed the neuroprocessor from the circuit. Then he took his tricorder off his belt and plugged the chip into an open slot.

"Tough break," muttered Lily.

"Yes." He couldn't worry about Lynch now. Picard adjusted his tricorder and watched the cryptic Borg graphics scroll across his tiny screen.

"We've got to get to the bridge." The captain jumped to his feet and rushed out of the holodeck, leaving Lily to chase after him.

# CHAPTER

# 8

Zefram Cochrane sat on a chunk of concrete and watched the people from the future go in and out of the missile silo. He didn't like the way they looked at him, as if he were some kind of freak. *They* were the freaks, not him.

When they looked at him, they weren't seeing a real person, but some character out of a history book. He didn't like it—it was just too weird.

"Doctor," said a voice.

He turned to see Geordi, the one with the strange eyes. Normally if a person had eyes like that, they were blind, but not this man from the future.

"Yeah?" grumbled Cochrane.

"Will you take a look at this?" Geordi handed him a handheld computer, which they called a *padd*. "I tried to reconstruct the intermix chamber from what I remember from school. Tell me if I got it right."

Cochrane stared at him. "You learned this in *school?*"

"Yeah," said Geordi cheerfully. "Basic warp design is a required course at the Academy. The first chapter's called 'Zefram Cochrane.'"

Cochrane only glanced at the padd. "Well, it looks like you got it right—"

They were interrupted by a tall gawky fellow who handed Geordi a section of copper tubing. "Commander, this is what we're thinking of using to replace the damaged warp plasma conduit."

While Geordi studied the tubing, the thin man kept staring nervously at Cochrane. "Fine," said Geordi, "but you've got to reinforce the copper tubing with a nano-polymer."

He handed the tube back to the man, who just kept staring at Cochrane. "Doctor, I . . . I know this sounds silly, but . . . can I shake your hand?" he stammered.

With a sigh, Cochrane let the man pump his hand.

"Thank you, Doctor!" he gushed. "I can't tell you what an honor it is to be working with you on this project. I never imagined I'd be meeting the man who invented warp drive. I mean, it's a . . ."

"Reg," said Geordi, cutting him off.

The man smiled sheepishly. "Oh, right . . . sorry. Thank you!" He hurried off.

"That's Barclay," explained Geordi. "He's the excitable type."

"What do you mean?" grumbled Cochrane. "They're *all* like that. They all act like I'm *special?*"

"I can't say I blame them," said Geordi. "We all grew up hearing about what you did—or what you're about to do. You know, I probably shouldn't be telling you this, but I went to Zefram Cochrane High School."

"Oh, really?" Cochrane thought he would be sick to his stomach.

Geordi looked around the bombed-out encampment. "I wish I had a picture of this."

"What?"

"Well, in the future this whole area becomes an historical monument. You're standing in almost the exact spot where your statue is going to be. On your statue you're looking up at the sky, with your hand sort of reaching toward the future."

Cochrane's stomach was really churning now. "Excuse me, I've got to go to the bathroom."

"Sure!" said Geordi cheerfully.

Cochrane walked slowly until he was out of sight of Geordi and the rest of his busy workers. He made sure that no one was following him, then he ran off into the forest as fast as he could.

Captain Picard opened a hatch in the Jefferies Tube and stuck his head up into the bridge. He saw the barrels of three phaser rifles pointed at his forehead. Luckily, they were manned by Worf, Hawk, and Beverly Crusher.

Beverly gasped with surprise. "Jean-Luc, we thought you were—"

"Reports of my assimilation have been greatly exaggerated." Picard smiled at Beverly. "I found something you lost."

He climbed out of the tube and helped Lily out. Lily nodded at all of them, but the only one she looked at was Worf.

"I'm Klingon," he explained.

She nodded, staring in awe at the bridge of the *Enterprise.*

"Report," ordered Picard.

"The Borg control over half the ship," said Worf. "We've been trying to restore power to the bridge and the weapons systems, but we've been unsuccessful."

Beverly frowned. "So far, there are sixty-seven people missing, including Data."

Picard's lips thinned at this grim news. "We have to assume they've been assimilated. Unfortunately, we have a bigger problem. I accessed a Borg neuro-processor, and I think I've discovered what they're trying to do. They're turning the deflector dish into an interplexing beacon."

"Interplexing beacon?" asked Hawk.

"A kind of subspace transmitter. It links all of the Borg together to form a single consciousness. If the Borg on this ship activate the beacon, they'll make contact with the other Borg in this century."

Beverly frowned. "But in the twenty-first century, the Borg are still in the Delta quadrant."

"They'll send reinforcements," said the captain.

"Humanity would be an easy target. Attack Earth in the past . . . to assimilate the future."

"We must destroy the deflector dish before they activate the beacon," declared Worf.

"We can't get to deflector control or a shuttle-craft," said Picard grimly. Suddenly he had an idea. "Mr. Worf, do you remember your zero-g combat training?"

The Klingon frowned. "I remember it made me sick to my stomach. What are you suggesting?"

"I think it's time we went for a little stroll," answered Picard with a smile.

Geordi felt terrible about letting Zefram Cochrane escape. But who would have thought that the greatest hero of the twenty-first century would turn out to be . . . a coward?

Most heroes weren't born that way, Geordi told himself. It took some major event to turn them into heroes. Very few of them ever saw it coming. Cochrane was a man who did his work in secret, without fanfare. And they had spoiled the secret and given him too much fanfare.

They should have approached him differently, but it was too late now. He, Riker, and a dozen other Starfleet officers were searching the dense woods for Cochrane. What would they do when they found him? Could you *force* somebody to be a hero?

Geordi stopped to look at his tricorder, and he picked up a lifesign in the forest. "Commander

Inside the Borg hive, Data watched with interest as two Borg workers added more human flesh to his face and arm. It was a fascinating process, one he might enjoy, if they weren't doing it against his will. The sensations were both pleasurable and painful.

After a while the Borg Queen slithered out of the shadows to check his progress. She looked pleased.

"Tell me," said Data, "are you using a polymer-based neuro-relay to transmit the organic nerve impulses to the central processor in my positronic net?"

She didn't answer. One of the Borg workers adjusted the restraint on his left leg. He watched to see how the restraints worked.

"If that is the case," he said, "how have you solved the problem of increased signal degradation inherent to organo-synthetic data transmission across a—"

"Do you always talk this much?" she snapped.

"Not always, but often."

She scowled. "Why do you insist on utilizing this primitive form of communication? Your android brain is capable of so much more."

He cocked his head. "Have you forgotten? I am endeavoring to become more human."

"Human!" she scoffed. "We used to be exactly like them. Flawed, weak, organic. But we evolved to include the synthetic, and now we use both to attain perfection. Your goal should be the same as ours."

"Believing oneself to be perfect is often a sign of a delusional mind."

"Small words from a small being." The Queen snarled. "You attack what you don't understand."

"I understand that you have no real interest in me," said Data. "Your goal is to obtain the encryption codes for the *Enterprise* computer."

"That is one of our goals," she agreed. "But in order to reach *our* goals, I am willing to help you reach *yours.*"

A Borg undid the restraint on his left arm in order to adjust it. While his arm was free, Data lashed out with his android strength and knocked the Borg across the room. He quickly started to break off the other restraints.

The Queen backed away as Data jumped to his feet. Two more Borg rushed at him, and he kicked one of them and punched the other. Escape was within reach, and he dashed to the doorway.

Halfway to the door, he ran into a forcefield that threw him back. Then another Borg rushed toward him with a sharp instrument. Data threw his arm in front of his face for protection, and the Borg's claw ripped open his new skin.

*The pain!* It was like nothing he had ever felt. He gripped his arm, watching the blood flow. More Borg surrounded him, but the Queen raised her hand to stop them. They froze in place.

"Is it becoming clear to you yet?" she asked. "Look at yourself, Data—standing there, cradling the new flesh I've given you. If it means nothing to you, why protect it?"

"I am simply . . . imitating the actions of humans."

She smiled coldly. "You're becoming more human all the time. Now you're learning how to lie."

He hesitated, confused. "My programming was not designed to process these sensations."

"Then tear the skin from your limbs," she said, moving closer. "Tear it off, like you would a defective circuit. Go ahead, Data. We won't stop you."

Data held his new skin, which was still throbbing with pain.

"Do it!" she ordered. "Don't be tempted by flesh."

But he couldn't tear it off. The Queen gently stroked the new skin on his face, and he felt more confused than ever. From the corner of his eye, he saw the plasma coolant tanks, and he remembered what he was supposed to do—destroy the Borg.

But he also thought about what it would be like to have real skin over his entire body. To feel pain, pleasure, sorrow, joy—this was what he had always wanted.

The Borg Queen wrapped her arms around him and kissed Data. He found it pleasant, and he kissed her back.

# CHAPTER 9

Picard, Worf, and Hawk stood in the cramped confines of the air lock, putting on their space suits. Picard pulled on his helmet and fastened it shut. The suits were lightweight and easy to move in, but it was still strange to hear his own breathing inside his helmet.

Worf handed Picard a phaser rifle, then gave one to Hawk. "I have remodulated the pulse emitters," said the Klingon. His voice sounded hollow, coming from a speaker inside Picard's helmet. "But we will only get one or two shots before the Borg adapt."

"Then we'll just have to make those shots count," answered Picard. "Magnetize."

Each of them touched a small control pad on the thigh of their suits. Picard heard a click as his boots became magnetized. It suddenly felt as if his feet were stuck in mud.

"Ready?"

Worf and Hawk nodded. Picard looked back at Lily, who was standing in the doorway of the air lock.

"Watch your caboose, Dix," said Lily with encouragement.

"I intend to." Picard touched the control panel on the wall, and the air lock door opened. Outside was nothing but the blackness of space, and the gleaming saucer section of the *Enterprise.*

As Picard led the way, he could hear the metallic clank of each plodding footstep. Because of the position of the air lock, they had to walk across the saucer upside down. Looking at the stars and the immense bluc planet only made him dizzy, so he tried to ignore them.

Their long shadows stretched across the curving plain as they made their way toward the deflector dish. Picard could hear Worf breathing heavily.

"Worf?" he asked. "How arc you doing?"

The big Klingon groaned. "Not good."

"Try not to look at the stars. Keep your eyes on the hull."

He could see Worf carefully watching his feet and nothing else. It seemed like forever that they walked upside down across the saucer section, but finally they climbed over a slope and saw the huge deflector dish. Picard's heart sank.

Six Borg were working inside the spoonlike structure, installing a crystalline device in the center of the dish. The machine had twelve long clear spines, and the Borg were charging them with power tubes. As the Borg worked, one of the spines lit up and changed positions. If they didn't act quickly, thought Picard, it would be too late.

"We should bring reinforcements," suggested Worf.

"There's no time," said Picard. "It looks like they're building the beacon right over the particle emitter."

Hawk lifted his rifle. "If we set our phasers to full power—"

"No," snapped Picard. "We can't risk hitting the dish itself. It's charged with antiprotons—we'd destroy half the ship."

"There are six Borg," said Worf. "I would not suggest a direct assault."

"No," agreed Picard. "But if each of us opens a maglock, we could release the dish from the ship."

Worf and Hawk looked at him as if he were crazy, but neither one of them had a better idea.

"Hawk, take number one. Worf, number three. I'll take two. Let's move out."

Worf and Picard set out in one direction, and Hawk in the other direction. They carefully skirted around the huge dish, trying not to alert the Borg. Picard reached his position when he saw Worf stop and hold on to his stomach.

"Mr. Worf," said Picard, "you're not going to vomit in there. That's an order."

"Aye, sir." Worf moved off toward maglock three.

In the distance, he could see Hawk bend over a deck plate and pull it open. With any luck, they would accomplish their mission without the Borg even noticing them. When Picard looked back at the Borg machine, he saw there were three spires now lit. They had to hurry!

He tried not to make a sound, but he couldn't help his boots clanking across the metal surface. He finally reached a deck plate that was labeled MAGLOCK PORTAL ONE. He knelt down and popped it open, revealing a web of Starfleet circuits and control panels.

Suddenly the six Borg stopped what they were doing and turned to look at the intruders. Three Borg split off and walked toward the men on the maglocks, while the others kept working. If a single Borg was successful in stopping even one of them, thought Picard, they would fail. All three maglocks had to be released.

Picard worked furiously, but there were several safety mechanisms he had to override. The deflector dish wasn't supposed to come off easily. He looked up to see a Borg walking toward him in a calm deliberate manner. It was a terrifying sight.

Picard glanced at Hawk, who was the closest one to the Borg. One of them was almost on top of him before he looked up. Hawk quickly drew his phaser and blasted the Borg in the chest. The creature went skidding across the saucer in a shower of sparks and flew into space.

Another Borg instantly stopped working and headed toward Hawk.

Worf, with his strength, was faring better. The big Klingon pulled the release lever on the maglock, and the deflector dish trembled beneath their feet. His actions were just in time, because a Borg was almost on top of him.

"The magnetic constrictors are disengaged!" reported Worf. He whirled and fired at the advancing Borg, but the beam bounced off his shield.

"They've adapted!" shouted Worf. The Klingon backed up, forcing the Borg to come after him.

Picard held up his useless phaser and watched a Borg steadily approaching him. Then he got an idea! When the Borg was within a few meters, he fired at the hull. Instantly a jet of high-pressure gas shot out and knocked the Borg backward.

That gave Picard a few more precious seconds, and he kept working. He looked at the Borg machine in the deflector dish and saw more spines lighting up. The Borg device was almost activated!

He glanced at Lieutenant Hawk and saw that the second Borg was almost on top of him. "Hawk!" he warned.

But it was too late. The Borg grabbed Hawk and dragged the human out of sight. Picard could hear the man's screams echoing in his helmet.

He saw Worf in the distance, fighting the Borg. The big Klingon drew a Bat'leth sword from a sheath on his back. He slashed at the Borg's forearm and cut it off, and sparks and blood shot everywhere. The arm started to float away, but it was stuck to the Borg by a long piece of tubing.

They continued to fight, and Worf finally plunged his sword into the Borg and killed him. But it wasn't a total victory.

"The leg of my suit is ripped," said the Klingon gravely. "I have only forty-five seconds of air."

Hawk was gone, and Worf was doomed.

The captain overrode the last safety mechanism and pulled on the hydraulic lever. There was a rumble within the ship as the second of the three maglocks was depressurized. On a screen inside the maglock, two words kept flashing: CYCLE INCOMPLETE.

Picard looked at Hawk's maglock, which was still closed, and he knew he had to get to it. He took a couple of steps toward it, but a Borg moved to block his way. There was no way for him to get past the creature. The Borg activated a whirring sawlike device on his hand and came after Picard.

At the same time the Borg machine lit up in the center of the deflector dish. Only two spires were still dark! Once they completed the beacon, they could send for a whole fleet of Borg to attack the Earth.

Without time to think, Picard reached down and hit the magnetic control on his thigh. There was an ominous click as his boots demagnetized, and Picard bent his knees and pushed off the side of the open deck plate.

Weightless, he went sailing through space, into the

gas cloud and over the Borg's head. Picard hoped his aim was true as he sailed toward maglock number three. He twisted around and tried to stop spinning.

The hull loomed in front of him, and he crashed into it. Somehow, he held on and managed to magnetize his boots again. With relief, his feet clamped onto the metal and held him steady. He reached down into the open access panel and finished Hawk's work. With all his strength he pulled on the lever and released the lock.

Bolts exploded all around the outside of the deflector dish, and Picard braced himself. As the dish began to move, the Borg looked up to see what was happening. The entire deflector dish separated from the ship and began to float into space.

Suddenly the dish stopped floating when the power cables stretched to their full length. Now the Borg were working furiously to finish their connections, and the dish glowed with tremendous power. Picard drew his phaser rifle and took careful aim at the cables.

Before he could fire, Hawk suddenly rose up and grabbed him! Only it wasn't Hawk, because he was now a *Borg!* The newest Borg forced Picard onto his back and began banging on the faceplate of his helmet. His faceplate began to crack under the blows, and Picard wasn't strong enough to stop him. Hawk raised his hand for one final blow.

Then a phaser blast caught Hawk in his chest and propelled him into space, tumbling and turning. Picard whirled around to see Worf. He was all right! Tied around his leg was a makeshift tourniquet made from Borg tubing and a Borg arm. It was a strange but welcome sight.

The deflector dish glowed, and the spines were blinking in unison. The Borg stepped back, done with their job, and Picard lifted his phaser rifle and took aim. He fired into the mass of power cables, and they exploded in a shower of sparks.

The deflector dish went dark and floated off into space, with the Borg still clinging to it. When it was about fifty meters away, Worf lifted his phaser rifle and took aim.

"Assimilate this!" he growled. He raked the dish with phaser fire, and it exploded in a fireball of metal and debris.

Grinning in victory, the Klingon looked at Picard. The captain smiled back, thinking that now they had a chance to stop the Borg.

In the Borg hive, the Queen suddenly jerked, and a twisted look came over her face. She gazed silently at the other Borg, and several of them hurried out of the room.

She walked to the operating table and looked at her prisoner. "We've had a change of plans, Data."

Inside the cramped cockpit of the *Phoenix,* Zefram Cochrane sat in the pilot's chair, facing upward. He stared at a complex bank of switches, dials, and readouts. In the doorway a security guard stood watch, making sure he didn't escape again. Cochrane tried to relax, but it wasn't easy.

Commander Riker climbed into the cockpit and sat down in one of the other two chairs.

"We've only got an hour to go, Doc," said Riker. "How are you feeling?"

"I have a four-alarm hangover," muttered Cochrane. "Either from the whiskey, or your laser beam, or both. But I'm ready to make history."

Riker smiled as Deanna Troi's voice broke in on the intercom. "Troi to Commander Riker."

He pushed a button. "Riker here."

"We're ready to open the launch door," said Troi.

Riker looked at Cochrane, who shrugged. At this point they might as well go for it.

"Go ahead," said Riker.

With a rumbling sound the silo door slid open, and both men watched through the cockpit window. They were looking straight up into the blue sky of morning, and the moon was still visible. It looked inviting, as if it wanted them to come out and play.

"Look at that," said Riker in awe.

"What?" asked Cochrane. "You don't have a moon in the twenty-fourth century?"

"Sure we do. . . . It just looks a lot different. Fifty million people live on the moon in my time. You can see Tycho City, New Berlin, and even Lake Armstrong on a day like this."

Cochrane stared at the white crescent, trying to imagine it with cities, lakes, and lights.

"And you know, Doctor—"

"Please don't tell me it's all thanks to *me*. I've heard enough about the great Zefram Cochrane." He checked the navigational computer, but Riker continued to look at him with disappointment.

"Listen," said Cochrane, "I don't know who wrote your history books, or where you got your information—but you people have some pretty funny ideas about me. You look at me like I'm some kind of a saint or a visionary."

"I don't think you're a saint," said Riker, "but you did have a vision. And now we're sitting in it."

Cochrane laughed at him. "Do you know what my vision is? Dollar signs. Money. There's still an economy out there, you know. There may not be any gold left in Fort Knox, but there's tons of cash overseas. Do you know how much the Indonesian Space Agency would pay for a faster-than-light rocket?"

"I can't imagine."

"Maybe you can't, but I can! I didn't build this ship to usher in a new era for humanity. I built this ship so I could retire to some tropical island, with lots of money. That's Zefram Cochrane . . . that's his *vision.*"

He ran a diagnostic on the computer. "This other guy you keep talking about—this historical figure—I've never met him."

Riker looked thoughtful for a moment. "Someone once said, 'Don't try to be a great man . . . just be a man. Let history make its own judgments.'"

"Nonsense," scoffed Cochrane.

Riker smiled. *"You* said it. About ten years from now." As Cochrane's mouth dropped open, Riker pointed to his clipboard. "Fifty-eight minutes, Doc. Better get back to that checklist."

The man from the future crawled out of the cockpit, leaving Cochrane alone. He rubbed his eyes, thinking about statues and high schools—all bearing his name. Well, if they were so desperate for heroes that they had to make one out of him, that was their business.

Picard and Worf strode onto the bridge of the *Enterprise.* Beverly Crusher, Lily Sloane, and the rest of the bridge crew looked at them with relief.

"We stopped them," said Picard, "but we lost Hawk."

Worf staggered a bit, and Beverly looked at him with concern. "Commander, are you feeling—"

"Hold that thought." Worf ducked behind a console and vomited.

Picard looked at Beverly and shrugged. "Strong heart, weak stomach."

"They're on the move again," said Beverly. "The Borg just overran three of our defense checkpoints, and they've taken Decks Five and Six. They've adapted to every modulation of our weapons—it's like we're shooting blanks."

Picard nodded grimly. "We'll keep working on a new way to modify our phasers. In the meantime, tell our people to stand their ground. Fight hand-to-hand, if they have to."

Beverly went to issue the order.

"Wait," said Worf. "Captain, I suggest we activate the auto-destruct sequence. We can use the escape pods to evacuate the ship."

"No," said Picard.

Beverly looked intently at him. "Jean-Luc, if we destroy the ship, we'll destroy the Borg."

The captain's jaw tightened. "We are going to stay and fight."

"We have lost the *Enterprise,*" growled Worf. "We should not sacrifice more—"

"We have *not* lost the *Enterprise,*" snapped Picard. "And we're not going to lose the *Enterprise.* Not to the Borg, and not while I'm in command." He turned to the others. "You have your orders."

Worf lowered his voice. "Captain, I must object to this course of action."

"Your objection has been noted, Mr. Worf."

The Klingon struggled to control his temper. "With all due respect, sir, I believe you are allowing your personal experience with the Borg to influence your judgment."

Picard was not going to have anybody tell him what to do with *his* ship. "I never thought I'd hear myself say this, Worf, but I actually think you're afraid. You want to destroy the ship and run away."

"Jean-Luc—" said Beverly, but Picard cut her off with a quick motion of his hand.

Worf continued to glare at him. "If you were any other man, I would kill you where you stand."

"Get off my bridge!" snapped Picard.

Worf balled his hands into fists, but he didn't strike

the captain. Instead he turned and stalked off the bridge.

Picard looked at the shocked faces of his crew. "You have your orders. We fight to the last man."

The captain turned and strode into the observation lounge.

# CHAPTER 10

Captain Picard sat by himself at the table in the observation lounge. He had two objects in front of him—a phaser rifle, stripped apart, and the Borg neuro-processor, hooked to a diagnostic device. He was looking for clues in the neural chip on how to modulate the phasers to work against the enemy.

The door whooshed open, and Lily stormed into the room. "You hypocrite!" she shouted.

"Lily, this isn't really the time—"

She wasn't going to back down. "Look, I don't know jack about the twenty-fourth century, but I do know that everyone out there thinks that staying here and fighting the Borg is *suicide*. They're just too afraid to come in here and say it!"

"The crew is accustomed to following my orders," said Picard evenly.

"They're probably accustomed to your orders making sense."

"None of them understand the Borg as I do," said Picard slowly. "Six years ago, I was assimilated into the Collective. I had their cybernetic devices implanted throughout my body. I was linked to the hive mind. Every trace of individuality was erased—I was one of *them.*"

"I am such an idiot," said Lily, sitting down across from him. "It's so simple—this is about *revenge.* The Borg hurt you, and now you're trying to hurt them back."

Picard scowled. "In my century we don't succumb to revenge. We have a more evolved sensibility."

"Yeah, right. I saw the look on your face when you shot those Borg on the holodeck. You were almost enjoying it."

He glared at her. "How dare you—get out!"

"Or what?" she sneered. "You'll kill me like you killed Ensign Lynch."

"There was no way to save him."

"You didn't even try," said Lily. "Where was your 'evolved sensibility' then?"

This was not a conversation that Picard wanted to have. "I don't have time for this—"

"Oh, hey, sorry. I didn't mean to interrupt your little quest. Captain Ahab has to go hunt his whale."

"What?" he snapped.

"Don't you have books in the twenty-fourth century?" asked Lily, leaning back in her chair.

"This is not about revenge!" declared Picard. "This is about saving the future of humanity."

"Then blow up this ship!"

"No!" Picard exploded with anger and threw his phaser rifle across the lounge. It smashed into a glass case, spilling models of previous *Enterprise* ships all over the deck.

"I will not give up the *Enterprise!*" declared Picard. "We've made too many compromises already, too many retreats. They invade our space, and we fall back. They assimilate entire worlds, and we fall back. Not again! The line must be drawn here—this far and no further! I will make them pay for what they've done."

Lily shrunk back from him, surprised at his passion. She looked down at the broken models on the deck. "You broke your ships."

Picard took a sharp breath and gazed out the window at the vast starscape. Yes, he had lost the *Enterprise-D,* and he didn't want to lose another ship. But maybe it was more than that—something more personal.

Lily started for the door. "See you around, Ahab."

Picard's noble voice cut through the silence. " 'He piled upon the whale's white hump the sum of all the rage and hate felt by his whole race. If his chest had been a cannon, he would've shot his heart upon it.' "

Lily stopped in the doorway. "What?"

*"Moby Dick."*

She gave him an embarrassed smile. "Actually . . . I never read it."

"Ahab spent years hunting the white whale that crippled him," said Picard. "It *was* a quest for vengeance. In the end, the whale destroyed him—and his ship."

"I guess *that* Ahab didn't know when to quit."

Picard's eyes narrowed as he thought about her words. Then he strode past her onto the bridge.

At his arrival, Beverly and the others stopped what they were doing and looked at him.

"Prepare to evacuate the *Enterprise,*" ordered the captain.

Cochrane, Riker, and Geordi strapped themselves into the reclining seats in the *Phoenix* cockpit. Cochrane took a deep breath and tried to remember everything he had to do. But then he remembered that Geordi and Riker knew his flight plan better than he did. They had probably studied it in kindergarten.

He flipped a switch. "ATR setting?"

"Active," reported Geordi.

"Main bus?"

"Ready," said Riker.

"Initiate pre-ignition sequence," said Cochrane.

The ship shuddered as the thrusters on the tail began to spew nitrogen gas.

Troi's voice broke in over the intercom. "Control to *Phoenix,* your internal readings look good. Final launch sequence checks are complete. You're at the thirty-second mark. Good luck."

"Thanks," said Cochrane.

Riker clapped his hands. "Everyone ready to make a little history?"

"Always am," said Geordi cheerfully.

Cochrane looked concerned. "I think I'm forgetting something—"

"What?" asked Riker impatiently.

"I'm not sure. It's probably nothing." Cochrane looked around the cockpit.

"Fifteen seconds," said Troi on the intercom. "Begin ignition sequence."

The rumble got louder, and the ship began to shake.

"Oh, yes!" said Cochrane. "Now I remember. Where is it?"

He began searching his pockets frantically, while Riker and Geordi looked on with concern. Troi's voice started the countdown. "Ten . . . nine . . . eight—"

"What . . . what?" asked Geordi.

"We can't lift off without it," said Cochrane.

Riker rolled his eyes. "Okay, Geordi, let's abort—"

"No, no wait! I found it!" Cochrane whipped out a small optical disc, which he punched into a slot on the control panel.

Deanna's voice continued the countdown. "Four . . . three . . . two . . . one!"

As the roar of the engines filled the cabin, loud rock-and-roll music blasted from the stereo. Cochrane grinned at his amazed companions. "Let's rock!"

The rocket engines ignited at full blast, and the converted missile began to rise from the silo. With his favorite rock song blaring over the speakers, Cochrane hardly noticed the roar of the rockets and all the shaking. They were on their way!

Flames shot from the rockets, and the missile zoomed out of the silo and rose into the air.

As they passed through the Earth's atmosphere, the ship really shuddered and shook. Cochrane gripped his joystick with white knuckles, and he looked at his companions. Both Riker and Geordi were perfectly calm, as if they did this every day. Of course, they really *did* do this every day.

"Can you turn down the music a little?" asked Riker.

Cochrane took a deep breath and lowered the volume. Suddenly the g-forces pushed them all back into their seats.

"There's a red light on the second intake valve," said Geordi.

"Ignore it," answered Cochrane. "We'll be fine. Prepare for first-stage shutdown and separation on my mark. Three . . . two . . . one . . . mark!"

The first-stage booster separated from the ship and dropped away. With a flash it burned up in the atmosphere. A moment later two sheets of metal fell away, and two primitive warp nacelles slowly extended from the ship. Finally, the *Phoenix* began to look like a starship.

The shaking inside the ship suddenly stopped, and Riker checked the controls. "All right, let's bring the warp core on-line."

But Zefram Cochrane didn't respond—he was too busy staring out the window at the millions of stars. Riker noticed the look and nudged Geordi.

"Wow!" was all Cochrane could say.

Riker grinned. "You ain't seen nothin' yet."

Picard sat stiffly in his captain's chair. "Computer, this is Captain Jean-Luc Picard. Begin auto-destruct sequence—authorization Picard one-one-zero-alpha."

There were only two other people left on the bridge—Dr. Crusher and Lieutenant Commander Worf. Both of them looked somber.

"Computer," said Beverly, "this is Commander Beverly Crusher. Confirm auto-destruct sequence—authorization Crusher two-two-beta."

They looked expectantly at Worf, who said, "This is Lieutenant Commander Worf. Confirm auto-destruct sequence—authorization Worf three-three-gamma."

The efficient computer voice responded, "Command authorizations accepted. Awaiting final code to begin countdown."

Picard took a deep breath and looked around at his

bridge. He could tell from the blinking consoles that most of his officers were already in their escape pods. Their destination was an uninhabited island on Earth named Gravett Island. It wouldn't be like living in space, but it was better than dying.

"This is Captain Picard," he continued gravely. "Destruct sequence one-A, in fifteen minutes. Silent countdown. Enable."

"Self-destruct in fourteen minutes, fifty-five seconds," answered the computer. "There will be no further audio warnings."

Beverly looked down sadly. "So much for the *Enterprise-E.*"

"I barely knew her," said Picard.

"I wonder if they'll build an *F?*" she asked.

Picard managed a smile. "I have a feeling they'll keep building them until they run out of letters."

Beverly and Worf started for the Jefferies Tube that would take them to the escape pods.

"Mr. Worf?" said the captain. The Klingon turned to face him. "I regret some of the things I said to you earlier."

"Some?" asked Worf with a smile.

Picard smiled back and warmly shook the Klingon's hand. "In case there's any doubt, you're the bravest man I've ever met. See you on Gravett Island."

Worf nodded, then he slipped into the Jefferies Tube, leaving Picard alone on the bridge. The captain looked around at his sparkling new bridge, which was about to become space dust. It was too soon to lose this ship, he thought sadly. And that feeling had nothing to do with the Borg.

Suddenly Picard heard the whisper of Borg voices in his mind, and he struggled to shut them out. Then a single voice cut through the din. *Captain,* it said.

"Data!" Picard gasped.

# CHAPTER
## 11

Picard hurried through the evacuation corridor. Hatches on the escape pods were closing all around him; there were only two still open—his and Lily Sloane's. The Earth woman stood in front of her escape pod, waiting for him.

"Lily," he said, "you're the only one going back to Montana. If you see Commander Riker or any of my crew, give them this." He handed her a padd.

"What is it?" she asked.

"Orders to find a quiet corner of North America, and stay out of history's way."

She sighed. "Well, good luck."

"To both of us." Picard started off down the corridor.

"Hey!" called Lily. "You're not leaving, are you?"

"No, I'm not," he admitted. "When I was held captive aboard the Borg ship, my crew risked everything to save me. I have a friend who's still on *this* ship. I owe him the same."

"Go find your friend," said Lily with an encouraging smile.

The captain gently pushed her into her escape pod and shut the door behind her. He made sure that all of the survivors were safely in their pods. Then he walked to the master control panel and pulled the lever. Fifteen escape pods shot into space and tumbled toward Earth.

*This is it,* thought Picard. He was going down with his ship, as captains had since the beginning of history. They could use Data's escape pod, if he saved the android in time.

Picard dropped from a Jefferies Tube into the corridor outside Main Engineering. It was still choked with Borg machinery, and the voices screeched louder than ever in his head. Picard didn't try to shut the voices out—he followed them to the Borg hive.

Two Borg suddenly stepped in front of him and blocked his way. Picard wondered how he was going to get past them, when they stepped aside. They were letting him into the hive, Picard realized. They wanted him to come.

The doors to Engineering slid open at his approach, and the voices in his head abruptly stopped. He didn't want to be this close to the hive again, but he forced himself to go inside. He had unfinished business with the Borg.

Inside the hive it was eerily quiet. Many of the Borg were in their chambers, asleep. Others were working the consoles, probably trying to override the auto-destruct sequence. There was no sign of Data, but he had a feeling that the android was here. A very strong feeling.

Suddenly there was a rustling, and a figure slid forward from the dark hoses and tubes at the back of the room. Picard gasped when he saw who it was—the dark-haired woman from his nightmares! The Queen! Picard wanted to run, but he froze in his tracks.

"What's wrong, Locutus?" she purred. "Don't you recognize me? Organic minds are such fragile things. How could you forget me so quickly?"

Picard staggered back, with the memories overwhelming him. He stared at the Queen with a mixture of shock and realization.

"You can still hear our song," said the Queen.

"Yes . . . I remember you." Picard gasped. "You were there. You were there the entire time! But that ship and all the Borg on it were destroyed."

She scoffed. "You think in such three-dimensional terms. How small you've become. Data understands me. Don't you, Data?"

Data stepped out of one of the boxes along the wall. Only it wasn't Data anymore! He was *human*. His hair was real, his skin was real, and his gold eyes were *blue*. Little Pinocchio was a real boy.

"What have you done to him?" asked Picard.

"Given him what he's always wanted," answered the Queen. "Flesh and blood."

"Let him go," said Picard. "He's not the one you want."

"Are you *offering* yourself to us?" she asked eagerly.

Picard nodded in amazement. "Offering myself . . . that's it. I remember now! It wasn't enough to assimilate me, you wanted me to give myself freely to the Borg—to *you!*"

"You flatter yourself," she said disdainfully. "I have overseen the assimilation of countless millions. You were no different."

"You're lying. You wanted *more* than just another Borg drone. You wanted the best of both worlds—a human being with a mind of his own who could bridge the gulf between humanity and the Borg. You wanted a counterpart, an equal. But I resisted; I fought you."

The Borg Queen narrowed her eyes at him. "You cannot begin to imagine the life you denied yourself."

"It's not too late," said Picard. "Locutus can still be with you, just as you wanted him. An equal. Let Data go, and I will take my place at your side, willingly, without resistance."

She caressed his cheek, and Picard felt like throwing up. He forced himself not to move as she touched him. "Such a noble creature," said the Queen. "A quality we sometimes lack. We will add your distinctiveness to our own. Welcome home, Locutus."

She looked at Data. "You're free to go. The force-field has been removed."

Data cocked his head, but he didn't move.

"Data, go," said Picard.

"No. I do not wish to go."

The Queen smiled with satisfaction. "As you can see, I've already found an equal. Data, deactivate the self-destruct sequence."

Picard swallowed hard. Data had the knowledge to deactivate it. But would he do it? When Data moved toward a console, the captain rushed to stop him, but two Borg grabbed him.

"Data! Don't do it!" shouted Picard. "Listen to me!"

Data ignored him as he struggled. His fingers were a blur as they worked the computer console. "Auto-destruct sequence deactivated," said the android.

The Queen smiled at Picard in victory. With Data on her side, there was nothing he could do to stop them. The Borg would survive, and they would have the *Enterprise*. With the *Enterprise,* they could easily defeat this primitive Earth.

"Now," said the Queen, "enter the encryption codes and give me computer control."

Data obeyed. Picard struggled to get free, but the two Borg held him tightly. Within seconds, all of the consoles in Engineering suddenly lit up, and the warp core started pulsing with power.

Data motioned to Picard. "He will make an excellent drone."

"Now we must destroy Zefram Cochrane's warp ship," said the Queen.

Picard started to protest, but the Borg covered his mouth and dragged him away.

At that moment the *Phoenix* was picking up speed, and Zefram Cochrane was starting to enjoy the flight. Maybe he did deserve to be a hero for building a warp ship out of an old missile. He looked at Geordi and Riker, and they both smiled at him.

"Plasma injectors are on-line," said Geordi. "Everything's looking good. I think we're ready."

Riker checked a clock on the instrument panel. "They should be out there right about now. We need to break the warp barrier within the next five minutes if we're going to get their attention."

"Nacelles are charged and ready," reported Geordi.

"Let's do it," agreed Riker.

Both of them looked expectantly at Cochrane. He nodded and said, "Engage."

The warp nacelles flared with power, and the tiny ship surged forward. "Warp field looks good," reported Geordi. "Structural integrity is holding."

Riker studied the instrument panel. "Speed is twenty thousand kilometers per second."

Suddenly a huge spaceship loomed outside the port window, making Cochrane jump. It was the same ship he had seen through the telescope—the *Enterprise.*

"Aren't they a little close?" he asked.

"Relax, Doctor," said Riker with a smile. "They're just here to give us a send-off."

In the Borg hive, Picard was tossed on top of an operating table. One Borg held him down, while another approached with a whirring needlelike instrument in his hand. Picard glanced at Data, who was still manning the console, still obeying the Queen. The situation looked hopeless.

"I am bringing the external sensors on-line," said Data.

The Queen stepped out of the shadows, smiling. She walked over to Picard and looked down at him, as a human might look at a bug.

"Excellent," she said.

Picard glanced back at Data, and the android looked up. Their eyes met briefly. Maybe it was only his imagination, but he thought he saw something of the old Data for a second. It gave him hope.

The cockpit of the *Phoenix* was shaking like a milk-shake blender as they picked up speed. Cochrane gripped the joystick with both hands, suddenly getting nervous again. What if the ship fell apart when they hit warp? What if it didn't work at all?

Then he looked at the two relaxed astronauts beside him. *Remember, Zefram Cochrane High School*, he told himself.

"Thirty seconds to warp threshold," said Riker. "Approaching light speed."

Geordi glanced out the window at the *Enterprise*, which was soaring along beside them. "They are getting pretty close. I wonder what they're doing?"

The tiny ship was really shaking now, and Cochrane gulped. "We're at critical velocity!"

Inside the Borg hive, Data continued to operate the

computer. Picard craned his neck and could see the *Phoenix* on the console screen. It looked as if Data was taking aim.

"Quantum torpedoes locked," said the android.

The Borg Queen nodded. "Destroy them."

Data hit the console and launched three powerful torpedoes at the tiny warp ship. Picard struggled against his bonds, but there was nothing he could do to stop him. Data began moving toward the warp core.

The Queen studied the viewscreen triumphantly. "Watch your future's end!"

But the torpedoes did not find their target—they sped past the *Phoenix!* Picard could see terrible anger in the eyes of the Borg Queen.

"Data!" she snarled.

"Resistance is futile," said Data. He whirled around and punched his fist into one of the plasma coolant tanks. A huge explosion of gas shot from the rupture, knocking Data halfway across the room. Smoke and deadly gas filled the hive, and the Borg held up their hands for protection.

Picard was suddenly free! He saw the Borg Queen look anxiously at her rescue system on the ceiling, and the cables began to descend. The captain jumped on top of the operating table and hurled himself at the Queen's cables. Desperately, he climbed the cables, trying to escape the deadly gas.

The Queen grabbed another cable, and it lifted her out of danger. She stared at the cable in Picard's hands, and it suddenly started to whip around, hurling him back and forth. The cable smashed Picard into the Queen, and somehow he held on.

Meanwhile, the *Phoenix* stretched like a rubber band and shot into space. For the first time in history, an Earth vessel entered warp drive. Cochrane was slammed back in his seat, and he watched the stars turn into streaks.

"Whoooa-a-a-a-a!" he shouted with delight.

Picard fought to hold on to the twisting cable. Below him, he saw flesh melting off the faces of the Borg as they died horribly in the gas. He tried to hold on, but the cable whipped around like a tiger's tail.

The Queen glared at him, and the cable began to wrap around Picard's arms and legs. He struggled— but he couldn't climb higher, and he couldn't break free. He began slipping downward, toward the deadly gas.

The Queen reached out a hand and grabbed his leg, trying to force him down faster. Picard kicked at her, but the cables squeezed his legs like a boa constrictor. His boot hit the rising gas, and the leather hissed and melted away. Picard prepared himself to die.

Suddenly a hand rose from the gas and grabbed the Queen. It was Data! Half the flesh on the android's face and arm was eaten away. With his android strength, Data shook the Queen, and she fell off with a shriek. Both of them disappeared into the deadly clouds of gas.

The cables went limp around Picard, and he climbed higher, to safety. He looked down to see the

Queen writhing in agony, dissolving in the gas. Data lay beside her.

Picard climbed to the third level of Engineering and jumped off onto a catwalk. A Borg moved to cut him off, but the creature began to twitch and stagger. Picard got around him and rushed to the wall panel. He hit the ventilation control.

With a sucking sound, the gas flowed out of the room into the *Enterprise's* waste system. He looked down, hoping it wasn't too late for Data.

There were Borg lying everywhere, dead, with all of their organic parts eaten away. Picard quickly scrambled down a ladder and ran to help his friend. Data was sitting up, but his human skin was mostly gone, leaving only bare metal and circuits.

Picard still heard the voices of the Borg in his head, and Borg were coming out of their boxes on the upper level. He rushed to the Borg Queen, who was nothing but a metal skeleton. As long as she lived, she could control the rest of the Borg.

She struggled to sit up, and Picard grabbed her metal spinal cord and snapped it in half. At once, she died, and the voices stopped. Borg on the upper levels of the hive stopped in their tracks, and the lights went dim behind their eyes.

Picard helped Data to his feet. "Are you all right?"

The android paused a moment to check his condition. "I would imagine I look worse than I feel."

The android glanced at the dead Queen. "Strange," he said. "Part of me is sorry that she is dead."

"She was unique," agreed Picard.

"She brought me closer to humanity than I ever thought possible," said Data. "And for a time I was tempted by her offer."

"How long a time?"

"Zero-point-eight-six seconds," answered Data.

"For an android, that is nearly an eternity." Picard smiled at his friend, and the two of them walked through the smoking ruins of Engineering.

Aboard the *Phoenix,* everyone was wearing a big smile. "That should be enough," said Riker. "Throttle back, and bring us out of warp."

"No problem," said Cochrane confidently. As he turned the ship around, a large star appeared in the distance.

"Is that Earth?" he asked in shock.

"That's it," answered Geordi.

Cochrane shook his head. "It's so . . . small."

"It's about to get a whole lot bigger," said Riker with a grin.

# CHAPTER
# 12

It was night at the missile complex in Montana, but men, women, and children stepped out of their shacks and tents. They stared at the sky, where the clouds were glowing with an eerie green light. Suddenly a huge alien ship broke through the clouds and lowered slowly to the ground.

The people walked toward the amazing sight, their faces reflecting their awe and surprise. They had seen war, missiles, and atomic bombs, but they had never seen anything like this.

A small group of people stood off to the side. Picard, Riker, Geordi, Deanna, Barclay, and the other Starfleet officers watched with satisfaction. Cochrane and Lily Sloane stood there with their jaws hanging open. Even though they knew this event was about to happen, seeing the glowing green ship was still a shock.

With its engines whining, the pulsing ship settled down to Earth. The engines stopped, and the crowd continued to surge forward, to see what would happen next.

Riker looked at Geordi, and the two of them gently took Cochrane's arms and pushed him forward. His spine tingled, and he felt sick to his stomach. But he knew destiny when he saw it—and this was his destiny.

"Doctor," said Geordi with a smile, "you're on."

Cochrane gulped, unable to move. "My God . . . they're really from another world?"

Riker nodded. "And they want to meet the man who flew that warp ship."

There was a mechanical click and a hiss of air as the hatch slowly opened. Cochrane took a deep breath and gathered all of the courage within him. He thought about taking a drink, but then he remembered that he had thrown his bottle away. No more booze for him.

He walked up to the ship and stopped, as the hatch opened all the way. Three hooded figures emerged from the ship and walked slowly down the ramp. He couldn't see their faces, and he wondered if they were bug-eyed aliens with six arms. Or would they be like humans?

They stopped in front of him and pushed the hoods

off their faces. They had pointed ears, slanted eye-brows, and pale skin, but they didn't look like monsters. Cochrane smiled, but they didn't smile back. They looked sort of serious.

One of them lifted his hand and spread his fingers in a strange way. "Live long and prosper," said the Vulcan.

"Um . . . thanks," said Cochrane.

The Vulcan cocked his eyebrow in a quizzical manner.

Picard nodded to Riker. "I think it's time we make a discreet exit."

The first officer walked away to round up his team, leaving the captain standing beside Lily.

She smiled at him. "I envy you, the world you're going to."

"I envy *you,* taking these first steps into the unknown."

"Might've been fun to take them together," said Lily with a twinkle in her eye.

"I'll miss you, Lily." Their eyes caught for a moment, and Picard reached out to her. They held hands, until finally Lily nodded and walked away. Like Picard, she was a realist.

The captain took his place with the rest of his crew and tapped his comm badge. "Picard to *Enterprise.* Energize."

Aboard the bridge of the *Enterprise,* Picard strode to the captain's seat and sat down. He looked at Data on the Conn. The android's face was still partially metallic, but he seemed to have suffered no serious aftereffects.

"Report."

Worf answered, "The moon's gravitational field obscured our warp signature. The Vulcans did not detect us."

The captain nodded, and Geordi said, "I've reconfigured our warp field to match the chronometric readings of the Borg sphere."

"Recreate the vortex, Commander."

"Aye, sir."

"All decks report ready," said Riker.

"Helm standing by," said Data.

The captain nodded. "Lay in a course for the twenty-fourth century, Mr. Data."

"Course laid in, sir."

The captain smiled inwardly. This was one time when he would give himself a "Well done." He pointed his finger at the viewscreen and said, "Make it so."

The swirling vortex opened in space, and the *Enterprise* soared through it, heading for home.

Down on Earth, Lily looked up into the night sky, and she saw what looked like a tiny shooting star. She imagined that it was her new friends, giving her a last thrill. She hadn't been on the flight of the *Phoenix* with Cochrane, but she had been on the *Enterprise*.

Suddenly the peaceful night was shattered by the

jangled chords of Cochrane's favorite rock-and-roll song. She looked back at the bar and saw him showing the jukebox to the Vulcans. It was hard to tell what they liked, but they were interested in everything.

The townspeople gathered around the door, watching respectfully. They knew this was the start of something big.

# About the Author

John Vornholt was born in Marion, Ohio, and knew he wanted to write science fiction when he discovered Doc Savage novels and the words of Edgar Rice Burroughs. But somehow he wrote nonfiction and television scripts for many years, including animated series such as *Dennis the Menace, Ghostbusters,* and *Super Mario Brothers.* He was also an actor and playwright, with several published plays to his credit.

John didn't get back to his first love—writing SF—until 1989, with the publication of his first Star Trek Next Generation novel, *Masks.* He wrote two more, *Contamination* and *War Drums;* a classic Trek novel, *Sanctuary;* and a Deep Space Nine novel, *Antimatter.* For young readers, he's also written three other Starfleet Academy books, *Crossfire, Capture the Flag* and *Aftershock,* plus *The Tale of the Ghost Riders,* an "Are You Afraid of the Dark?" book. All of these titles are available from Pocket Books.

John is also the author of several nonfiction books for kids and the novel *The Witching Well.*

John lives in Tucson, Arizona, with his wife, Nancy, his children, Sarah and Eric, and his dog, Bessie.

# BLAST OFF ON NEW ADVENTURES FOR THE YOUNGER READER!

Pocket Books presents two new young adult series based on the hit television shows, STAR TREK: THE NEXT GENERATION® and STAR TREK: DEEP SPACE NINE®

*Before they became officers aboard the U.S.S. Enterprise™, your favorite characters struggled through the Academy....*

## STAR TREK
### THE NEXT GENERATION®
## STARFLEET ACADEMY®

**#1: WORF'S FIRST ADVENTURE**
**#2: LINE OF FIRE**
**#3: SURVIVAL**
by Peter David

**#4: CAPTURE THE FLAG**
by John Vornholt

**#5: ATLANTIS STATION**
by V.E. Mitchell

**#6: MYSTERY OF THE MISSING CREW**
**#7: SECRET OF THE LIZARD PEOPLE**
by Michael Jan Friedman

**#8: STARFALL**
**#9: NOVA COMMAND**
by Brad and Barbara Strickland

**#10: LOYALTIES**
by Patricia Barnes-Svarney

**#11: CROSSFIRE**
by John Vornholt

**Published by Pocket Books**                    928-10